CONFESS TO DR. MORELLE

A pretty girl and a drunken producer are involved in a dramatic motor accident on the road from Lyons to Paris — a fruitful source for blackmail. The first sinister consequence occurs at a party where, among the actresses and producers, Dr. Morelle is present with his secretary, Miss Frayle. The famous criminologist finds himself plunged into one of the strangest cases of his career as he takes to the airwaves to unmask a murderer before he can kill again!

ERNEST DUDLEY

CONFESS TO DR. MORELLE

Complete and Unabridged

LINFORD
Leicester

First Linford Edition
published 2005

British Library CIP Data

Dudley, Ernest
    Confess to Dr. Morelle.—Large print ed.—
Linford mystery library
1. Morelle, Doctor (Fictitious character)
—Fiction 2. Detective and mystery stories
3. Large type books
I. Title
823.9′14 [F]

ISBN 1–84617–034–6

Published by
F. A. Thorpe (Publishing)
Anstey, Leicestershire

Set by Words & Graphics Ltd.
Anstey, Leicestershire
Printed and bound in Great Britain by
T. J. International Ltd., Padstow, Cornwall

This book is printed on acid-free paper

1

The girl was walking alone.

The star-filled sky turned the road into a white ribbon unwinding endlessly ahead of her. Not a car in sight, no camions, no noisy French motor-bicycles. No one to give her a lift.

It was past midnight. The girl quickened her pace. Her shoes were not suitable for this sort of trudging. But the friction of her shoe against her heel gave her a savage sort of satisfaction. Almost it eased the burning shame in her heart as the thoughts twisted sickeningly round in the old groove. A gramophone-record that wouldn't be switched off.

Fool, she told herself. Stupid little fool. Did you imagine it was your conversation he was interested in? Her mouth twisted at the joke, but her eyes were bitter.

It all rose up again in her mind so that she had to fight back a physical nausea. It had started so well. The thrill of the flight from Northolt, late at night, the arrival at Orly at three in the morning. Her first sight of Paris, a sleeping Paris, with the street-lights burning silently, the wide empty boulevards. Raoul had taken her into a café and they'd had the *café noir* and calvados.

She tasted again the sharp burning flavour of the calvados. It had made her gasp, brought tears to her eyes, and he had watched her intently, had put his hand over hers and laughed. She should have seen it then. She should have known.

They had drifted around Paris, hand in hand, until the dawn. He had pointed the sights out to her, but with her head spinning with the need for sleep and the effects of the calvados, she had been too dazed to follow the way they had taken. She remembered the imposing U.N. building, she remembered staring up at the gaunt skeleton of the Tour Eiffel, with a fierce wind whipping at her skirts. 'It's always windy here,' Raoul had said. 'We'll go up it, when we get back to Paris.'

They had wandered down dark canyon-like streets, with the blank shuttered windows, to her so curiously foreign-looking. Along the left bank of the river, where all the little bookstalls huddled against the river wall, and she stared up fascinated at the looming solemn mass of Notre-Dame.

They had crossed and re-crossed the Seine. Pont Neuf, Pont St. Michel and the Palais de Justice; and Pont Sully. They were a blurred memory to her now, these old wide stone bridges of Paris, with the dark silent Seine flowing underneath.

Raoul had talked; this had been the Raoul she loved. Talkative and amusing, full of knowledge about Paris, full of warm gaiety.

And when Paris woke, and the streets burst open, scattering men and women from the Metro and the buses as a ripe seedpod scatters its multitude of seeds, Raoul had taken her to this café in a narrow side-street, where they had breakfasted on brioches and coffee and fruit. Raoul had winked at the woman who served them and told her what were obviously outrageous stories, in French.

Then the thick-set swarthy man had come in, and Raoul had introduced him. 'This is Diana. This is Michel.' And Michel had talked to her and Raoul about London in very good English. He had given Raoul the keys of the Simca and told him not to drive the car too fast because she was not so young now and she must be treated carefully.

Presently Raoul had taken her to a little garage in the back street and there was the Simca, battered-looking and in need of a respray. It was to take them South, to Marseilles, Raoul had given quite a comic performance, reversing the car out into the street and cursing at a man with a handcart who would not get out of the way.

They had talked over this for so long. He had tried so hard to persuade her to come, to convince her that it would be an adventure, a wonderful way of discovering his beloved France. And because she was only nineteen and romantic, she had read into his insistence something that had never been there.

She had lapped it all up. She had truly believed that he wanted her to know and love France, because he did. She had visualized a time when he would ask her to marry him, to live in France with him. She had dreamed that at the end of this holiday he would ask her to marry him.

But it hadn't been like that at all.

They had headed South in hilarious excitement. Even when Raoul had started to step on it, and kept his foot down good and hard and she'd been nervous, after a while the thrill of speed entered her blood. She had stared avidly at the countryside whizzing past, the terrain south of Paris, with its small towns, the tall façades of houses and hotels, and farms and rivers.

She had watched Raoul's hands on the wheel, his narrowed eyes fixed on the road which leapt at them. They had lunched at a restaurant which did not look like a restaurant, but more like an old mansion set back from the road, with gardens that flanked a quiet-flowing river. She was remembering now the *escallope de veaux*, the *salade de tomatoes*, the sickly-sweet *marron-glaces*.

They had lunched at a little table by the river, and she threw bread-crumbs to a fat, lazy trout which flickered watchfully just under the surface of the water. Wine with the lunch a *vin blanc*, and black coffee. Afterwards they had driven on through the heat of the afternoon, until suddenly Raoul had pulled the car off the road into a lane and announced abruptly that he wanted to sleep.

By a half-completed hayrick in the corner of the field he had thrown off his jacket and within two minutes was asleep. Half-piqued, half-amused, Diana had sat watching him. Unease had stirred in her, but she could not trace its cause. She got up and walked to the top of a little hill. The terrain had changed now, and instead of the vaguely familiar pattern of fields and farms, she looked across rolling stretches of vineyards, steep wooded slopes.

High on a distant peak of rock, an old chateâu looked as if it belonged to medieval French chivalry. Dark on the hillside were forests of conifers, sombre against the brilliant green of the vine-yards. A breath-taking panorama, and she stood quite still for a long time looking at it.

When she returned to where Raoul lay, it was as though he had heard her footsteps on the dry grass, he suddenly sat up. He woke up quickly, instantly he was alert and smiling. He found cigarettes and lighted two. 'Do you like it?' he asked.

She took a cigarette. 'It's beautiful.'

'We are on the way to Lyons,' he said. 'Where I was born. That's why it's to be our first place to stop at.' He was on his feet. 'We shall never make it if we don't get a move on. Come on.'

They drove on through a golden land, where the roads climbed up above steeply dropping valleys; a village where children stood in a silent huddle round the car when Raoul stopped for petrol.

'Not far now,' he said. She dozed on the seat beside him. Once her head fell onto his shoulder and he made no attempt to move it. Then he was shaking her gently. 'Diana. We're here.'

It was big, much bigger than she had expected, a great sun-filled mellow city, jostling and bustling in the early evening. They were driving slowly over one of its two great bridges, with the river Saône far beneath them, wide as the Thames at Waterloo, when for the first time she wondered about the arrangements for their stay. She had left all the travel arrangements to Raoul, had been content to do so. 'Where are we staying?'

'An hotel,' he had said. Was his tone suddenly evasive, then? He had pointed to a great stone building. 'First job I ever had was there. I worked in a tiny little office right up at the top.' He had laughed. 'Can you imagine me in an insurance company?'

He had pulled sharply off the wide street and turned into a narrow one. Abruptly the smooth road-surface gave way to bumpy cobbles. 'Good Lord,' she said. 'Wherever are you taking me?' She was smiling, but he did not answer. He wrenched the wheel round and slewed the car into the narrow entrance alongside a little hotel.

'Our first *port d'escale.*' He sounded light-hearted, but had there been a tenseness in his face? The engine roared in the confined yard. Expertly he backed the car into a corner, switched off the engine. He leaned across the girl and opened her door, and she saw that he was grinning, his eyes glittering with amusement. Diana got out of the car silently and stood waiting while Raoul pulled their suitcases out of the boot. The place looked dilapidated, the paint on the outside of the windows was blistered, one of the shutters hung crookedly from a broken window frame.

As though aware of her dismay, he put an arm across her shoulders. 'One of the first things you have to learn about French hotels,' he said, 'is that they always look beastly from the outside. The second thing I'll explain to you in a minute.'

She followed him inside, frowning at his last cryptic remark. There was a small glass-windowed office, and inside sat a large, elderly woman in an outmoded tight black silk dress. Her greying hair was twisted up into an untidy knot on the top of her head. She wore rimless spectacles close against her faded eyes. When Raoul reached the little window of the office she looked up, disinterestedly. He launched into a stream of French. The woman eyed her shrewdly, so that Diana blushed and was angry with herself for doing so. The woman looked hard at Raoul, who laughed and he held out his hand for the keys.

The woman shrugged, reached for a big brass key from a hook on the wall and handed it to Raoul.

'Shouldn't there be another?' Diana heard herself say, and her voice sounded tremulous in her ears.

Raoul grinned at her blandly. 'Let's go up the stairs, it's only two floors,' he said, and grabbing the two suitcases, went on up the circular, rickety staircase. Diana followed. There was in her nostrils for the first time the smell of all cheap French hotels. The smell of Gaullois cigarettes mingled with the faint odour of lavatories. Now she wrinkled her nose. On the second landing Raoul stopped. There was a narrow passage, uncarpeted, with white-painted doors on either side. He pushed the key into the lock of one of the doors.

She followed him into the room, her heart thumping. It was rather bare, with windows that looked across the narrow street to the shuttered windows of a house opposite. In one corner of the room was a wash-basin, in another corner an old wardrobe. There were two straw-bottomed chairs, one of which was as frayed as a year-old bird's nest. And in the centre of the far wall was a big double-bed.

Diana stared at it, ashamed, frightened. Then bitter anger filled her. She lifted her eyes to Raoul's face. He was watching her. What was it in his face? Triumph?

It was in that instant that, only half-knowing what it was, she experienced a premonition, a flash of foresight that she was staring at someone who was an inhuman stranger, a monster who was not beyond anything, however desperate or evil if it suited his purpose.

2

The feeling vanished as he came across the room to her. He put his arms round her and pulled her close to him. Tipping up her chin he began to kiss her. For a moment she struggled, then she felt limp in his arms. She had often thought of him kissing her like this and the idea had been exciting, stirring. But now she was experiencing only revulsion.

When he released her she found that she was no longer afraid. Quietly she went to where her suitcase lay. She opened it and took out a few things, wrapping them in a bundle she could carry.

'What are you doing?'

'Taking what I need. You can take the rest of my stuff back to Paris in the car.'

'For God's sake.' He sat down incredulously on the bed. 'What's all this?'

'I just don't want to stay, not like this.' She nodded towards the bed.

'Stop behaving like a schoolgirl and

grow up,' he said harshly. 'What did you expect? Two single rooms, and a key on the inside of the door?'

She fought back the panic which assailed her. She resisted the longing to cry, to let the scalding tears carry away the angry bitterness that filled her mind. She was in a strange place, somewhere she had never known in her life before. She had about four thousand francs on her, and she spoke very little French.

'Seems I wasted my time bringing you here, then.' He crossed to her, his lower lip stuck out.

'If that's what you wanted, yes I suppose so.'

Now she felt ridiculous, humiliated. She felt she was in fact behaving like a schoolgirl and it wasn't an attractive role. And she was hurt because he stood there scowling at her, instead of taking her gently in his arms and telling her that it was all right.

'We could have fun,' he said. 'You don't know what it is like. It makes two people close.' He spoke softly, his eyes bright. For a second she glanced at him and again that hint of fear touched her.

They stood looking at each other, he sullen-faced and angry, then she walked to the door. He said nothing. Slowly she turned the big brass door handle, waiting for him to call her back, to put it all right. But he did not speak, nor move.

She found herself on the bare landing. She stood listening then began to walk past shut doors off the landing. She thought she heard the muffled sound of a woman laughing somewhere, behind one of the closed doors. At the end of the passage she turned and looked back at the room. Now she wanted to go back, wanted desperately to see Raoul. But he didn't appear. What was he doing? Lying on the bed, smoking a cigarette, waiting for her to come back?

She looked down the twisting staircase. There was a faded carpet on it that had once been bright with red and yellow roses, but it was nearly threadbare. The odour of Gaullois cigarettes hung on the warm evening air.

Suddenly there was the bang of a door. She started as if it had been a revolver-shot. Then came a gabble of French from an upper landing, and children came racketing down the stairs. One, two, three, lanky French boys in shorts and wearing bow-ties and crew-cut hair, and an ugly dark little girl in a fussy dress, all bows and ribbons. Behind them came a short woman, fat and slow, apparently the children's mother.

The children had hardly noticed Diana, standing there quietly, but the woman smiled at her, eyes shrewd and appraising. '*Bon soir, m'selle. Fait-il chaud, dans votre chambre? La mienne, c'est terrible! Comme un four!*'

She went on down the stairs still chattering. Diana had said: '*Bon soir,*' then stood watching the children clatter their way to the bottom and out into the street. The hotel was quiet again, there was no sound from the direction of the room behind her. Slowly she started down the stairs.

She did not want to face the woman in the office, but when she got to the hall, no figure in black sat behind the glass-windows, it was empty. Almost furtively

15

she hurried past and out into the street.

It was mid-evening now and the sky was a warm luminous blue. Far to the west it was still barred with gold and the air trembled with the slightest of summer breezes. She walked along the street where they had come in the car, and then she stood, at a wide junction of streets, utterly at a loss.

One of the roads was the main thoroughfare which had brought them into the city. In the distance she could see the wide bridge which spanned the Rhône; away to her left appeared to be Lyon's main shopping section. The corner where she stood was a residential part, with hotels dotted between the high apartment-houses.

The streets were noisy with evening promenaders; music came from a nearby café, the inevitable accordion melody of a French radio-station with a sentimental tenor ah-ing and l'amour-ing to the tune.

She found herself at the door of the café. She saw little tables spread with blue and white checked tablecloths and along one side of the café a bar. She was too miserable now to be self-conscious and she went in and sat down at a table in the corner. There were a few people chatting and eating and the radio behind was going full blast. A young girl came to her table.

'*Vous voulez, mademoiselle?*'

'*Café noir.*' Then suddenly she realized she was hungry. She looked at the hand-written menu. 'And . . . *et une omelette espagnole.*'

When the omelette came she thought it bore little resemblance to the plain, beaten-egg concoctions she cooked in her bed-sitter in London. This smelt rich, there were fried onion-rings heaped on it, and when she cut it she identified potatoes, tomato, parsley, chives, even pimento. She ate ravenously and as she drank the strong black coffee, resolution returned. She would hitch-hike back to Paris, get home to London, forget all about Raoul.

She had learned her lesson.

She fought down the weak longing she felt for him. No doubt about it, she reflected wryly, she was half in love with him. But it was no good. She didn't want that kind of a relationship with him.

There remained the problem of where to spend the night. She shrank from the prospect of another third-rate hotel, and she decided there and then to start walking as long as she could, then try and find some barn or haystack where she could sleep till dawn. She paid her bill, remembered that the word *compris*, on the bill meant she didn't have to tip, and walked out into the warm evening.

Presently she was heading along the road that stretched back Paris-wards. She paused for a while on the bridge, leaned her arms on the stone parapet and stared down at the water. Then with a shiver, not of cold, she set off again.

It would be better, she thought, not to try for a lift at night. There were a lot of camions along the road, but they travelled non-stop and if one did stop for her she might be asking for trouble. Daytime it was different, auto-stopping was a recognized way of travel, it had its own code of behaviour.

Dusk fell swiftly. Her face turned

north, she walked on steadily if it had not been for the one painful memory of her parting with Raoul, she would have enjoyed it. Then quite suddenly it was dark. The road was wide, flanked by vineyards and woods; overhead the sky was bright with a myriad stars; traffic lessened, only occasionally did the glaring eyes of the camions come at her, roar close and then fade. The air freshened, a stiff breeze sprang up.

Diana stopped and untied her bundle, pulled out the leather jacket she had brought. It was comforting and she zipped it up under her chin gratefully, she began to think about a place to sleep. She noticed a lane leading away from the road, and far down it a barn of some kind. She turned off the road to investigate. The barn belonged, she discovered, to a rambling old stone house set back from the road, with farm buildings dotted round it.

The barn smelt richly of fruit, but it was empty. The floor was hard-packed earth and Diana looked at it dubiously, it would make a hard bed. Then she found a heap of sacks against one of the walls, they seemed to be clean and dry. There were about half-a-dozen and she used half for a mattress, the rest for blankets, with her clothes bundle for a pillow. As soon as she lay down and covered herself over, exhaustion flooded her and she fell asleep.

She awoke suddenly, her heart racing with an unknown fear. She realized where she was and made out the time by her wristwatch. It was past midnight, she had slept about three hours. She felt cramped and a little chilled. She decided to continue her journey, there was something about the silent, shadowy barn that scared her. That curious presentiment stabbed at her again, she couldn't think why or what it was. She was free of Raoul now, he couldn't harm her. Yet the fear persisted. She would feel safer out under the night-sky. She would push on until she was too tired, then snatch some sleep again.

An hour or so later, the now familiar never-ending woods and vineyards stretched on either side of her, the wide road stretched ahead, pale beneath the stars. The breeze was still fresh. There was very little traffic. It was then that she heard the car behind her. It sounded like a sports-car. She turned as it raced towards her. As it came out of the darkness, she thought she saw, with a lift at her heart, that it was an English car.

Impulsively she stepped out from the side of the road, a hand raised to stop it for a lift. The headlamps held her, blinding her with their glare, but the car didn't slacken speed. And it seemed to swerve as if out of control. A tremendous glare enveloped her.

Then all was blackness.

3

The man at the wheel of the M.G. pushed his foot down hard on the accelerator and watched the needle creep up; sixty, seventy, eighty. He narrowed his eyes to fix them on the road. The roar of the engine filled his ears, its tune familiar to him as the sound of his own heartbeats.

He was a skilful, reckless driver. He had nearly lost his life so many times, that he had begun to believe violent death was not meant for him. Only thing I can do, he'd tell himself cynically over and over, is drive a car. No nerves when I'm driving. The French roads had unwound before him since before dawn, towns strung out along them, Montelimar and Avignon, Nîmes and Montpellier, and always the blazing Van Gogh countryside, burning fields of ripe wheat and dark conifers.

He had roared out of Sète while the

22

fishing-port was still asleep and had driven hard. About five in the morning he had pulled up in a tiny village. The streets were empty, shutters still fastened, but his nose had sniffed the fragrance of hot new bread and he had tracked down the bake-house and persuaded them to sell him a new loaf, still too hot to eat; at seven he had pulled into a routiers café for coffee, and they had given him farm butter to put on his loaf; at midday he had paused briefly to buy fruit from a market stall.

He had dozed during the hot afternoon for three hours, under the shade of a tree, the whirring of the crickets in his ears. Then he had pushed on again and now it was evening and Lyons lay not so many kilos ahead. And there, he promised himself, he would have a slap-up dinner and a bottle of wine. The sense of elation that had buoyed him up ever since he set out was beginning to ebb. The thought of the money was no longer real. Almost he believed there had been some mistake.

Why should the old trout leave him her money? He'd never been a very dutiful nephew. She knew he was no good, would never amount to anything.

Perhaps that was why. She'd left it to him to spite the others, give them something to snarl about. He grinned and notched the needle up to eighty-five. At least he'd get more enjoyment out of it than they would. No tying it up in stocks and shares for him, no security, gilt-edged or otherwise. He'd have a damn good time with it and when it was gone, he'd be back where he started. So what?

The road curved. He took the corner too quickly, skidded, and fought the M.G. until he had it under control. 'Swine,' he swore between his teeth. 'Do what I damn well tell you.' His brown, heavy-featured face was wet with sweat, his soft, rather sensual lips were pressed into a tight line. The hands that gripped the wheel were exceptionally fine for a man, but they were strong, capable.

When the houses and shops began to race past him and he realized he was approaching the outskirts of Lyons, reluctantly he let the speed come down. Once in the Lyons traffic he picked his way cautiously, looking for a place to park the car while he ate. He found a promising-looking place, a modern-style restaurant, all plate-glass and chromium, with a fancy indoor garden of banked flowers at one end, and a well-stocked bar at the other.

It had its own car park, up a cobbled alley and when he left the M.G. he stretched his legs and walked into the restaurant. He didn't notice the man alone at the next table, who looked up and eyed him with sullen disinterest at first, then he stared at him. 'Guy Keaping, what are you doing in this part of the world?'

Guy Keaping looked at the lean, dark individual who had risen from his table. Then he grinned. 'Dassinget, isn't it? Raoul Dassinget?'

The other nodded vigorously as he moved towards Keaping. 'It is a small world. May I join you?'

Guy Keaping nodded. 'Surely.' They shook hands and sat down together. 'I've been holidaying in Marseilles, looking up a girl I used to know,' Keaping said. 'I'm on my way back to London.'

'By road?'

'It's an M.G. this time,' Keaping said. 'What was it in Paris that time? The Lagonda? Or had I sold it?'

'It was a Chev. You ran it into a wall the night we went to the Vieux Colombier, remember?'

'Oh, yes.' For a second his face clouded. He didn't like to be reminded of his mistakes, his failures.

'What are you doing these days?'

'Nothing much. I finished with the paper way back. I've gone and fixed myself up with a job in steam-radio.' Dassinget looked surprised. 'Yes, I know it's in its death-throes, and I rather it'd been television. But it was a job, so I took it. Now, as it happens I really don't mind it. One of my aunts went and died and left me a lot of dough. I'm on my way home to collect.'

'Lucky devil. Nothing like that ever happens to me.'

The girl came for Keaping's order. Dassinget noticed the soft, flattering smile he gave the girl and the way she caught her breath. He remembered the way Keaping always looked at a woman like that automatically. It made any woman twenty years old and beautiful. His eyes were warm and caressing, and yet with a shy quality that was infinitely appealing.

He ordered salad, and a steak and a bottle of vin ordinaire, when the food came he ate hungrily. Raoul joined him in the wine and Keaping ordered another bottle. As Raoul filled his glass again, he said: 'With your permission, I shall get drunk.'

Guy Keaping raised an eyebrow. 'Any particular reason?'

Raoul's face went dark. He set his glass down on the table.

'A woman?'

'A virgin.' Keaping had finished his steak and now he pushed the plate away. He refilled his own glass. 'I ought to have known better,' Raoul said gloomily. 'I brought her all the way from London, drove her down here, and the result, she walks out on me.'

'Where is she now?'

'Damned if I know. She's auto-stopping

her way back to Paris.'

Keaping looked at him curiously. 'Can she speak French? Has she any money?'

'She speaks the lousy French of an English schoolgirl.' Bitter frustration was in his voice. 'She's got a few thousand francs and a bundle of clothes. She left her suitcase with me, told me to take it back to Paris for her in the car.'

'A girl like that might run into trouble.'

The other shrugged. He filled his glass again. By now the second bottle was nearly empty. 'My car's packed it in, anyway. Exhaust-pipe's cracked. When I tried to drive it just now, I was nearly gassed by the fumes.'

'No business of mine,' Keaping said, 'but I don't like the idea of this girl being on her own. Look, why not come back with me? I'm going back to Paris. You could get your own car sent on.'

'Damn it,' Raoul said, 'it's her own fault. She ought to have known.'

'There are still a few innocent ones left,' Guy Keaping said dryly.

Raoul shrugged again and muttered, his speech a bit thick with the effects of the wine. However, he agreed to Keaping's plan.

He left the latter to settle the bill while he went off to make the necessary arrangements with the garage where he'd left the Simca. Keaping would wait for him in the M.G.

As Keaping waited in the car by the restaurant he wondered why he'd let himself in for this. Raoul Dassinget wasn't a particularly pleasant sort, and he'd obviously done this girl dirt. Keaping supposed it was because he himself was half drunk, morose and sorry for himself.

He found himself thinking back to when he had known Dassinget before, in Paris. He had been a mixed-up kid, then. Dassinget was working for U.N. Radio, translating and commentating. Keaping was in Paris to cover a scientific story for his paper, dull stuff that did not interest him, so that he had been glad of a chance to blow off steam when the day's work was done.

He and Dassinget had beat up the town between them, drunk too much, whored too much, driven too fast. It had culminated in Keaping's abrupt recall to London, a row with his editor, and then he had been sent to West Berlin. He knew it was his last chance. The knowledge soured him.

When he met Lise, the attractive wife of a café proprietor, he sent one last insolent cable back to London and went off with her into the Black Mountains.

Guy Keaping shrugged away the bitter memories. He lit another cigarette. The starry darkness was seeping into the narrow cobbled alley where he waited, and then he heard footsteps on the cobbles and Raoul Dassinget appeared, a suitcase in each hand. He strapped them onto the back of the M.G., fumbling and cursing, and got into the car. His face was moist with sweat, his eyes swivelled. With a spasm of irritation Keaping told himself this was what came of getting half-sozzled and chivalrously maudlin.

He switched on the ignition, pulled the starter, released the handbrake. He eased the M.G. out of the alley in low gear, fondled her round the sharp corner, wove through the streets and then let her out as the road widened and the traffic thinned. He may have been a bit fuddled, but it didn't get in his way of driving. The headlights sliced the darkness apart.

'What time she walk out on you?' he asked.

'About seven this evening.'

'She may have put up at an hotel.'

'You think I should have charged after her, don't you?' Wine and a bad conscience made him truculent.

'Somehow I don't think she'd accept a lift at night.'

Raoul slumped further down in the seat and his eyes closed. Keaping concentrated all he could on the road. He wished now that he hadn't drunk so much. He felt heavy, somnolent. He would have liked to follow his passenger's example and sleep. He knew he should pull off the road and doze for an hour. He grinned wryly. Chasing along an empty road at night looking for a girl he'd never seen, a girl Raoul hadn't even described. Except that she was a virgin.

Maybe there'd be a place where he

could get some coffee. Black, strong coffee. He became a part of the car, it was as if accelerator and clutch were an extension of his own limbs, linking him to the power underneath the bonnet. The steady throb of the engine drowned his thoughts and bore him along in a kind of wakeful coma. His eyes searched the dazzle of light ahead for this girl.

Once or twice he braked hard, thinking he had seen a solitary shadow, but when he got close it would be no one, and he would shake his head and push on.

The man beside him was asleep, his head sunk onto his chest, his mouth partly open; even when the M.G. cornered sharply he only rolled in the seat. Keaping's eyes had half closed, his hands were hooked on to the wheel. The road stretched ahead.

The road one moment was empty, the next moment his heavy eyelids widened instinctively as someone moved out from the side, waving. He had only time to see a face suddenly contract with horror.

His foot went down hard on the brake, he wrenched the wheel over, felt the car skid. The jerk threw him against the wheel. Raoul was flung forward and his head cracked against the windscreen. A ghostly dust, kicked up by the wheels, swirled round the car as it halted.

Dazed, Guy Keaping opened the door. He lurched out on to the road, what he saw made him retch.

The nearside wing of the car had struck the girl, flung her aside. One of her shoes lay in the road, the other was still on her foot. He stumbled across her as she lay, half on the road, half on the dusty grass. One side of her head was smashed in, one arm was a bloody pulp.

As he stared at her he saw that she was young. Scattered on the grass were a few clothes, a handbag lay open, a passport had fallen out of it. Automaton-like he went across and picked it up. He opened it with shaking fingers.

Name of bearer, he read, Miss Diana Margaret Morse. British Subject; Citizen of the United Kingdom and Colonies.

4

When Doug Blackwood spoke to her, Miss Frayle gave a start. She had been day-dreaming in the corner of the control-cubicle. Only vaguely she had heard someone put down the talk-back key to tell the actors in the studio that there was a ten minutes break before recording started.

Miss Frayle had never confessed it to anyone but Radio House hadn't been at all as she had imagined it. Everyone seemed to be so cynical and disillusioned. 'Steam-radio's had it,' that was the comment she heard on all sides; she'd heard the slim, heavy-featured man who was producing the show use that very phrase to Blackwood, he was the programme-engineer, before they had started rehearsing.

'What did you think about it, Miss Frayle?' Doug Blackwood asked her again.

'I think it's going to be splendid,' she said hastily.

He grinned at her and turned back to the slim man, who was saying to him: 'Did control-room like the level?'

'Okay, Guy, except when Ethel le Neve nearly knocked the needle off the dial in that last scene. I'll wind her back a few decibels next time.'

'She's hard to balance against Crippen. He's got that quiet, meek characterization pretty well.' And Guy Keaping glanced across at Miss Frayle for her approval.

She duly nodded, thinking that if only he wasn't like the others; he ought to be much more dedicated, almost. But to him it was just a job of work, with a pay-packet attached. She found it quite dispiriting.

She looked across at the girl who was playing the disk inserts, the headphones over her ears as she picked up her yellow wax marking-pencil and bent over the turntables. She had the job of fitting in the quick bursts of atmosphere music, recorded sound effects, all the seagoing atmosphere of the journey of the steamship *Montrose*, across the Atlantic. Like piecing together a jigsaw puzzle, with the sounds of the sea, the ship's engines, shipboard chatter; and the inevitable wireless message which had made criminological history.

Over the girl's head, in the string racks, were rows of gramophone effects records, numbered, marked. Carla Collins had the responsibility of playing them into their appropriate places in the script. Miss Frayle watched her admiringly. The deft way the girl plucked a disk down from the rack, plopped it onto spinning turntable, lowered the sapphire delicately onto the pencil-mark she had made in rehearsal, and listened to the record through her headphones.

Miss Frayle had once asked her if she could try, herself, and Carla Collins with her habitual insolent smile had handed her the headphones. 'Help yourself.' Miss Frayle's hand had trembled. She was afraid to lower the little handle which controlled the pick-up head, afraid she might injure the record. She had missed the beginning of the record, come in instead on the middle word of a sentence.

Carla had smirked. 'Now try and come in on the yellow wax mark.' Miss Frayle looked at the faint line marked some way in across the disk, then hesitated, helplessly. 'As near as you can by eye,' Carla said. 'Then adjust with the vernier scale.'

She'd pointed out the marked scale along the back of the turntable, and the wheel which moved the pick-up head. Miss Frayle hadn't the faintest idea what she was talking about. She'd twirled the mechanism in what she hoped was a professional manner and lowered the handle which controlled the pick-up head. She'd missed the yellow wax mark by about twenty grooves.

Carla Collins had taken the headphones from her ungraciously. 'I wouldn't call it a brilliant attempt.'

Miss Frayle eyed the girl now. Over-made-up, with her tight sweater, narrow skirt and spike heels. After her fumbled attempt at emulating her she had avoided Carla, then found she was to be the gramophone assistant for the Crippen feature.

Miss Frayle's new job had come about through Dr. Morelle's recommendation. Several weeks ago, a few days before he had left England on a tour of Scandinavian criminological centres, police bureaux and training-schools, Radio House had asked Dr. Morelle if he would act as adviser on a series of British trials they were recording for export abroad. Dr. Morelle's vast criminological knowledge would prove invaluable in presenting a balanced picture of the workings of British justice.

Regretfully declining, he had suggested Miss Frayle. With her knowledge and experience gained as his secretary she could, he had maintained, with unusual generosity, be very useful as technical assistant to the producer concerned.

Miss Frayle had been overwhelmed with pleasure when she'd heard about it. She had duly arrived at Radio House, she had stood staring up at the great white stone building, with its two hewn figures high above the entrance, then she had climbed the stone steps. Presently she had reported to the small sunny office six floors above the street where the slim, heavy-featured man had regarded her thoughtfully. 'I hope you won't find it dull here, after the more scintillating aura of 221b Harley Street.'

She had looked at the man uncertainly, and then he'd smiled the warmest smile any man had ever given her, and leaning across his desk took one of her hands in his. 'Welcome to Radio House, Miss Frayle.'

Now Guy Keaping put the talk-back key down again and called the studio. 'Stand-by now. We're going ahead in three minutes.'

Doug Blackwood had finished his engineering tests, he had sent line-up tone from studio to recording-room for them to check his output, he had spoken on the intercom to the recording engineer, telling him the expected duration, and had made a note of the recording numbers.

The programme was to be recorded both on disk and on tape. The tape was used for playing back into the station's own radio network, the disks were processed and sent abroad for overseas transmissions. The series had been rated as important, and the Radio House's top man had been assigned to it. Miss Frayle knew that though he'd been there barely two years Guy Keaping had fast achieved a reputation.

Writing and producing his own material, his scripts had an incisive, biting quality that cut sharply across a flood of second-rate material. Miss Frayle had seen him at work, seen how he wrestled with an idea until he had forced it into its most dramatic shape, and had seen him translate it into radio of thrilling impact.

Now that the moment of recording had come, Keaping's responsibility was almost over; it passed quietly and easily into the hands of the programme-engineer. And Doug Blackwood was on top of his job. Familiar with every aspect of radio production, subtly handling the rows of potentiometers on his control-panel to obtain every acoustic, every nuance of sound from his studio; never excited, immovable as rock, he remained as unimpressed by his own skill as a conjuror.

Miss Frayle watched Doug Blackwood lean forward. His eyes were on the second-hand of the clock, edging its way round the last minutes. Miss Frayle's heart began to race as he put the talk-back key down. 'Stand-by, studio and recording-room,' he said. 'We shall go ahead with this recording in ten seconds from . . . now.'

You could have touched the silence, Miss Frayle thought fancifully. Blackwood's hands were ready on the knobs, Keaping sat tense, his cigarette burning out unheeded in an ashtray. Carla Collins stood poised, waiting to play the introductory music. The cast, back in the studio were staring up through the glass panel at the control-cubicle. Then the red light. Blackwood said:

'Right, grams.'

Carla's hand came down and the introductory chords of music blared through the loudspeaker. Blackwood held them loud for a moment, faded them, cued the first actor and brought up the speech over the music. Slowly he took the music out. The actors in the studio got into their stride.

Miss Frayle relaxed. She saw the tense lines of Keaping's face loosen as he looked around for his cigarette, stubbed it out and lit another. Miss Frayle gulped and sat back in her chair. That first thirty seconds was agonizing. Keaping looked round at her. 'Cigarette?' he said. She shook her head with a smile.

She watched him give Carla a cigarette, hold the lighter to it. She noticed again, as she had noticed before, the fine, sun-tanned hand. He snapped the lighter shut, and then she found herself absorbed, familiar as it was to her, in the fateful career of Dr. Crippen.

The recording ended at six p.m. There was a general rush for Radio House's canteen and bar. Miss Frayle was undecided whether or not to go along with the others when Doug Blackwood took her arm. 'Come and have a snifter, Miss Frayle. And by the way, I'm throwing a bit of a party at my place. I hope you'll come.'

'I'd love to,' Miss Frayle said with pleasure. 'I love parties.'

They went into the canteen together, mingling with the actors and actresses Miss Frayle had only a brief while ago heard impersonating Dr. Crippen and Ethel le Neve, Inspector Dew and Belle Elmore.

She couldn't yet get over her amazement at the ease with which they adopted and discarded the characters they assumed. It was matched only by the incongruity of their physical appearances compared with their voices. The mild-mannered, astigmatic little Dr. Crippen had been played by a tall, willowy actor who specialized in American or Canadian accents, and who went to incredible pains to make sure that the accent he used was of the appropriate part of the American continent. The actress who'd given such a robust performance as the ill-fated Belle Elmore was by contrast a small, plump little woman of indeterminate age who looked like a school-teacher.

Miss Frayle found herself in a corner of

the bar which was a smallish space off the canteen. It was garishly-lit with bright green walls and glass-topped tables and green wicker chairs set round. The hubbub of voices grew louder as more people from the Crippen recording and other programmes drifted in relaxing from the taut nervous tension of the studio.

Although she had been at Radio House only a brief time Miss Frayle had already learned to spot the inevitable bores, the actor who was ever on the alert for an ear willing to listen to an interminable account of the numerous roles he had performed with such shattering success, or the gossiping, venomous-tongued young woman who had all the latest dirt on the current office-scandal. Like Betty Lewis, for example, whom Miss Frayle saw coming into the bar now. She was a junior programme engineer, who handled the spot effects on the programme.

Miss Frayle sighed a little. She didn't like the look of Betty Lewis at all. She watched her now as she thrust her way into the group about the bar, making some sharp comment to one of the actors who stood in her way.

The late summer's evening had turned sultry, heavy; despite the air-conditioning the atmosphere was threatening. The roar of London's traffic from the street far below came up muted and blurred. One of the curtains filled and blew inwards. A breath of air quivered in the room and died with a gasp. Miss Frayle felt grateful for the brief gulp of air as she waited for Doug Blackwood to bring her drink.

She had experienced an obscure sense of disappointment that Guy Keaping had not come along with the rest of the crowd. Some technicality, he had said wearily, some futile bit of paper he'd forgotten to sign. He had gone back up to his office. And then Blackwood came back with her drink. As soon as he had sat down next to her, other people shifted over to their table, as though attracted by his personality. Betty Lewis was one.'

'Little tramp,' she was saying, and Miss Frayle wondered who she was vilifying this time. 'I really can't think why she hasn't been sacked before now. I mean, with all this cutting down of staff.'

'She's a good disk player,' someone said drily, and Miss Frayle knew that the object of Betty Lewis's venom must be Carla Collins. The Lewis girl gave a bitter little laugh.

'Maybe, but she's a tart. Anyway, I hear Raoul's dropped her.'

'She's had a good run for his money,' Doug Blackwood said.

'That's a joke,' Betty Lewis said. 'He doesn't give any money. He's a taker only.'

Miss Frayle sipped her drink uneasily. Betty Lewis was referring to Raoul Dassinget, who worked with a unit broadcasting French programmes. Miss Frayle hadn't met him, but he seemed to possess an unenviable reputation. Doug Blackwood had caught her expression. 'Does all this kind of thing shock you, Miss Frayle?' he said in an undertone. 'Not quite what you're used to, I imagine.'

Miss Frayle took a little umbrage at being accused of leading a sheltered, innocent life. She said airily: 'Oh, I don't know, my job with Dr. Morelle has taken me into a few odd situations.'

'You sit watching, and you don't say very much,' Blackwood said. 'Storing it all up in that pretty little head of yours, no doubt, as psychiatric fodder for your boss.'

She went pink. Over her horn-rimmed spectacles her eyes met his. She twirled the stem of her glass. 'What strikes me is the atmosphere of disillusion. As though none of you believed in what you are doing. Why not get a different kind of job?'

'We've all lived and breathed radio so long, most of us. There aren't many similar jobs to choose from. All we can do is continue to flog a dead horse.'

'There's television,' she started to say, but he laughed with some bitterness in his tone.

'Those who couldn't get into that racket went long ago. The rest are stuck with steam-radio till death do them part.'

'But there'll always be a place for radio, I mean, I don't think television could improve on this programme about Crippen.'

But he shook his head. 'What happened to silent films when talkies came in? This is the same thing.'

She saw him look at Betty Lewis, who was staring at herself in the mirror of her compact. She got out a brilliant lipstick and remade the outline of her mouth. She wasn't pretty, reflected Miss Frayle, but she had tremendous vitality.

Doug Blackwood was right in the way, Miss Frayle went on to decide privately, her job as Dr. Morelle's secretary had not brought her much into contact with her contemporaries. Not like this job, anyway. She felt curiously old-fashioned, set down in the midst of these bright, hard people.

Betty Lewis waved to a man who had just come in. He was about twenty, hollow-cheeked, hungry-looking. He stared at Miss Frayle, then said to Betty Lewis: 'When I've got my drink,' and went to the bar.

'Have you met Bill Scott?' Blackwood asked Miss Frayle, who shook her head.

'Knows everything there is to know about tape-machines.'

Betty Lewis turned to her, her eyes gleaming. 'He's mad about Carla. Crazy jealous of Raoul. She doesn't even know he's living.'

Miss Frayle deliberately turned to Doug Blackwood. All this about Raoul Dassinget and his reputation was over her head and she had no wish to be involved in the gossip.

The bar was filling up. Miss Frayle was wondering if Guy Keaping was going to show up, or if she would see him at the party, when Bill Scott came over and Blackwood introduced him to her. 'The famous Miss Frayle,' Betty Lewis said unnecessarily. 'Slumming while the eminent Dr. Morelle's away.'

Miss Frayle blushed with embarrassment. 'On the contrary,' she said quickly. 'I'm enjoying it here very much.'

'I only meant it as a joke,' Betty Lewis said, giving Miss Frayle an amused smile.

'I don't think Miss Frayle thought it was a very good one,' Bill Scott said and gulped his drink.

But Betty Lewis had lost interest in him as she saw someone come into the bar. 'Here's Raoul,' she said in a harsh whisper. 'Note the change of partners.'

So this was the notorious Raoul Dassinget. Miss Frayle eyed him with interest. Mid-twenties, lean, dark, restless eyes, nervous hands. She saw the woman who was with him, he had his hand at the back of her neck, as they waited at the bar. She was pressing herself close to him.

'Been going on for a couple of weeks,' Miss Frayle heard Betty Lewis behind her say through her teeth. 'But he'll be in trouble if Carla finds out.'

5

The woman with Raoul Dassinget was a singer named Maria Fox, she was married to a hot-tempered musician from Middle Europe. All this Miss Frayle deduced from the conversation about her as the two newcomers waited at the bar. Out of the corner of her eye Miss Frayle caught a convulsive movement from Bill Scott.

As Dassinget and the woman got their drinks and made for an empty table, everyone seemed to be watching them. Everyone except Doug Blackwood who, Miss Frayle observed, was watching Scott amusedly. Blackwood would despise dog-like devotion, useless yearning for the unattainable. He'd go out after what he wanted, she thought, and if he couldn't get it, he'd stop wanting it. He was powerful, in build and in potentiality.

Betty Lewis was muttering under her breath. 'Let him have his women,' was what it sounded like to Miss Frayle. 'They're cheap sluts, all of them.'

At any rate Bill Scott swung on her, his eyes glinting. 'You're jealous as hell of Carla. Always have been. Because men like her company. I don't blame her, I blame Raoul and I'll get my own back on the dirty swine.'

Doug Blackwood eyed him quizzically then his gaze shifted over his shoulder. 'Here comes your girl friend,' he said casually. 'You'd better go and hold her hand.'

Carla Collins and Guy Keaping came in and Miss Frayle felt an unreasonable pang. As soon as Carla saw Dassinget she left Keaping and moved quickly across to him. She was looking rather unkempt, with her shoulder-length dark hair, but still very attractive as she stopped before Dassinget and Maria Fox. The man looked up at her.

'Hello, Raoul,' Carla said clearly, her attitude taut as a bowstring. He said nothing, just grinned warily. 'I want to talk to you.'

'Sorry, darling. I'm busy now.'

The woman beside him gave a nervous giggle.

'It's important.'

He shrugged. 'Sorry, darling.'

'But I must see you. It's important, I tell you.' Her voice was pitched high. The bar was suddenly silent, all attention focussed on the trio in the corner.

'For goodness' sake.' Raoul stood up, his face streaky with anger. 'Leave me alone. Always wanting this and that. Want to go out. Want to stay in. Want to talk. Want to — ' He left it unfinished and turned his back on her. Maria Fox stared up at him uncertainly.

Miss Frayle heard Blackwood beside her gulp down his drink, as Carla, her face paper white, swayed on her feet, then she turned and went out. In the silence that followed Guy Keaping came across to Miss Frayle and said: 'I meant to ask you if you'd come with me to the party Doug Blackwood's giving to-night.'

Miss Frayle couldn't help wondering if she was an afterthought now that Carla Collins had gone, but he fixed her with his warm smile, and her heart gave a little flutter. She wasn't used to being looked at like that. 'Mr. Blackwood's already asked me,' she said. 'But of course, I'll come with you.'

It was about half-an-hour later when they all started to drift out of the bar and out of Radio House into the street. Miss Frayle accompanied Guy Keaping round to the car-park and got into his car, a low-slung sports saloon, and they were heading in the direction of Bayswater.

Doug Blackwood's place turned out to be a three-storey Georgian-style house that faced the Regent's Park Canal in Little Venice. Miss Frayle had heard about it from Keaping on the way there. How Blackwood's parties were quite famous. He lived far beyond the scale of an engineer at Radio House. He was reputed to have private money.

Presently Guy Keaping was steering Miss Frayle across the wide entrance-hall and into the room that lay to the right of it, furnished in contemporary style. Everywhere brilliant tones of red and black, which made Miss Frayle blink. There was one big stark painting on the wall. A nude woman with a guitar, so sensually painted that Miss Frayle looked away.

People had already arrived and were laughing, talking, smoking. An archway led through into the dining-room and kitchen combined. This had been converted into a bar for the occasion. Doug Blackwood was at a long table of bottles and decanters. 'What'll you have?' he asked Miss Frayle. 'No need to ask Guy. Not while the whisky lasts out.'

'Gin and tonic for me, please,' said Miss Frayle. It was what she'd drunk at the Radio House bar. She glanced round her, thinking how different all this was to 221b Harley Street. She sighed, where was Dr. Morelle at this moment? Was he, too, at some party, much more glamorous than this, of course? This party held a curious under-current of unease, as if someone was going to burst into hysterical laughter. Or something like that.

Miss Frayle's thoughts concentrated upon Dr. Morelle once more. Another week and he should be back. And she'd be back with him, her work at Radio

House completed. The next few days promised intensive recordings of the two more famous British murder trials scheduled, then it would all be through and her job a memory, a little interlude soon to be forgotten in the mass of work she'd have to cope with in Dr. Morelle's employ.

'All right if I help myself?' Guy Keaping was saying.

'Sure.' Blackwood pushed the whisky bottle over. He eyed the other with a hard look, and Miss Frayle thought she caught something in his manner which made her realize that he didn't like the other.

Keaping poured himself a stiff whisky and drank it as if he needed it. He seemed different, unhappy, morose. When Bill Scott came up and asked her, abruptly, to dance, Miss Frayle was glad. But Scott didn't turn out to be exactly bubbling over with fun either. All he could talk about was Carla; he took an unwilling Miss Frayle into his confidence to tell her what a generous, maligned girl Carla Collins was. He was worried about her, he said.

But before he could confide further he

was interrupted by a tap on the shoulder.

'Mind if I cut in? I should like the pleasure of a dance with Miss Frayle.'

It was Raoul Dassinget. Miss Frayle's heart gave a flutter of nervousness, while the other jerked away from his touch as though it was poisoned, and Miss Frayle saw him watch scowling as she was swept into the middle of the room by Dassinget, to the music from the long-playing record on the radiogram.

It was a waltz that had just started, and Dassinget held her very close. It seemed to her that everyone was watching, and she was very uncomfortable. She could not deny the Frenchman's magnetism. She felt as though an electric current was surging through her veins.

'Who would have thought I'd have the pleasure of dancing with the famous Miss Frayle?'

'I'm afraid mine is only reflected glory,' she said. 'If Dr. Morelle were here no one would notice me at all.'

His hand pressed into the small of her back. 'You are quite fascinating in your own right. You mustn't let yourself be overshadowed by anyone.'

She knew it was false flattery, but a glow went through her. Perhaps he wasn't so bad as everyone made out. Perhaps he did chase after women, but he was extremely charming to her. 'I hope you won't be annoyed with me if I give you a word of advice, Miss Frayle.'

She had been glancing round, wondering where Maria Fox had got to, but she couldn't see her. Perhaps the man who was holding her too close had come to the party alone? At his question, she looked up at him through her hornrims. 'What kind of advice?'

'I should warn you to steer clear of Keaping.'

She gazed at him in astonishment. 'He's been very kind to me,' she said, flustered, and hardly knowing how to reply.

His dark eyes gleamed down at her. Uncertainly she looked over to where the slim, heavy-featured figure stood by the drinks, with his glass of whisky. Over the rim of the glass he was staring at them. Anger in his face. Or something else. Concern? Miss Frayle could not be sure.

Then there was a hand on Dassinget's shoulder twisting him away from Miss Frayle. It was Blackwood. Beside him the other man looked puny. 'Clear off, Raoul,' he said, his tone pleasant, but incisive. 'It's my party and I want to dance with Miss Frayle.'

She couldn't help giggling to herself. Her head was quite turned with the excitement of it. A party, dancing, a stream of partners cutting in, she hadn't had such fun for a long time. What a pity Dr. Morelle wasn't around to see it all. Doug Blackwood was saying in her ear: 'See that?'

It was Carla Collins laughing hysterically, clutching on to Bill Scott. She had managed to change into a dress that was outrageous in dark red, cut so low Miss Frayle could hardly bear to look at it without blushing. Her long dark hair tumbled over her shoulders. The effect of her was breath-taking.

'I didn't expect her to show up,' Blackwood was saying, half to himself.

'After that business in the bar.' Miss Frayle saw that Bill Scott's face was bleak with misery.

Then the girl in red saw Raoul Dassinget. Miss Frayle watched her steady herself, thrust young Scott away. She walked across to the Frenchman as if each step hurt. Perhaps it did, Miss Frayle thought fancifully. She was walking into a future she didn't want. A future where Dassinget bored with her, embraced other women. Carla was speaking loudly, thickly, to the rest of the room. 'I know what you're thinking. Raoul and I are washed up. But you're wrong. Aren't they, Raoul?'

'You're drunk, Carla,' Dassinget said, his tone level. 'Better get someone to take you home.'

'Drunk? Of course I am. And who's to blame if I am?' Miss Frayle saw Maria Fox appear out of a group by the door. So she had come with Dassinget, he hadn't arrived alone. It was Carla Collins who'd come alone. The pretty, baby-faced singer suddenly stepped forward. 'Why don't you leave him alone?' she said shrilly.

'He's sick and tired of you.'

'Keep out of this.' Carla moved forward. 'Raoul, tell this bitch to go back to her husband. If he still wants her after — '

Miss Frayle looked away, and saw on the other side of the room Guy Keaping suddenly grinning. As though Carla Collins had also seen the grin, she swung round to Keaping. 'You,' she said fiercely, 'you tell Raoul he'd better not turn me down. Maybe he'll understand, then.' Miss Frayle intercepted the curious look that flashed between the two men. Dassinget made a quick movement with his hand as though to silence the girl in red.

The tension broke for no apparent reason, except perhaps that it had held too long. People shrugged, turned back to their conversations, their drinks.

Miss Frayle noticed that Dassinget was smouldering, he had been made to look a fool and he knew it. Not the great lover. Just a man with two quarrelling women. He thrust Maria Fox, who had moved to him, away, glared at Carla, then turned and pushed his way from the room.

Blackwood was dancing again with Miss Frayle. 'What a damn fool he is, involving himself with bickering women. Thought Carla had more sense, too.'

'Perhaps she's desperate,' Miss Frayle said.

'About what?'

But this Miss Frayle didn't know. A few moments afterwards some late arrivals came in noisily calling for drinks, and Doug Blackwood piloted Miss Frayle over to where Keaping had moved away from the array of bottles and gleaming decanters and stood by himself. He still had a glass of whisky in his hand.

'If you'll forgive me,' Blackwood said to Miss Frayle, 'I'd better cope with this lot.'

'Sure you can spare her for a few minutes?' Keaping said over the rim of his glass to the departing Blackwood's back as Miss Frayle joined him. He returned her look, and she thought there was an expression in his eyes she had not seen before. She frowned to herself.

'You haven't seen the rest of the house, have you?' he said abruptly. 'Let me show you round. Doug won't mind.'

They went up a wide, elegant staircase that led to the first floor. Miss Frayle observed the handsome proportions of the rooms upstairs. There was a sombre, almost monastic bedroom, and, across the landing, a wonderful panelled library, with french-windows opening onto a balcony.

'It looks out over the canal,' Keaping said. 'Let me show you.'

He opened the windows and stepped out on to the balcony. The evening sky was a dark blue; the closeness of the earlier evening had gone and a faint chill of impending autumn sharpened the air. The balcony faced across Blomfield Road, quiet now, and beyond ran the dark waters of the Regent's Park Canal, seen through a screen of tall trees. A slight breeze stirred the surface and set the reflected lights dancing. They stood in silence for a few minutes, looking out to the big silent houses on the other side of the canal.

'Penny for them?'

She had been lost in thought. Encouraged by his question, she ventured to ask him the question that was in her mind. 'What did she mean when she said you could make him understand that he ought to talk to her?'

She had barely got the words out when it was as if Guy Keaping had slammed a door shut. His face went blank; he raised his eyebrows. 'Did she say that?' he said. 'You must have misunderstood her.'

His tone was icy and Miss Frayle felt herself floundering. She felt as if the heavy-featured man beside her, together with the others: Dassinget, Bill Scott, Carla Collins and the Lewis girl were spinning a web round her, a web of silent innuendo and suspicion. Faintly from another room, came the sound of the Greenwich time-signal, and the voice of an announcer. It seemed to emanate from Blackwood's bedroom on the other side of the landing. Had he deserted the party to come upstairs to listen to the radio?

Or had he followed her and Keaping

for some reason, Miss Frayle wondered, in an attempt to eavesdrop, for instance? She told herself she was imagining things, and yet she wished she had left unsaid the question she had just asked.

6

The yellow Duesenberg purred along Notting Hill Gate, travelling east towards the Bayswater Road. Dr. Morelle was at the wheel, and in the garish glare of the overhead street lights his face appeared dark and saturnine. At the entrance to Queensway he turned left and rolled slowly down the wide thoroughfare, past the book-shops, the fruiterers, the delicatessen stores. From the great plate-glass windows of a big store wax figures grinned coquettishly out at him, their trim shapes clothed in autumn's coming fashions.

Held on the corner by traffic lights set to red, Dr. Morelle leaned back against the leather upholstery of the driving seat. He breathed deeply, inhaling the nostalgic smoky smell of the London night. He was not displeased to be back. The tour had been stimulating, he had received from his Scandinavian hosts a reception flattering enough to someone even of his eminence, and the social acclaim and hospitality accorded him had been everything that he could wish.

Moreover he had been able to air his views at length, he had spoken of his concept of the criminal mind and had heard his ideas, even his most revolutionary ones, upheld by the world's greatest psychologists and criminologists. A smile touched the edges of his finely chiselled mouth. Yes, the trip had in every way been a complete triumph.

The lights changed. Dr. Morelle set the car in gear and it slid smoothly forward. He turned right into Bishops Bridge Road, then almost immediately left across the great railway bridge outside Paddington Station. From below him came the shriek of a train-whistle, and a billow of steam swirled up over the span of the bridge. For a moment Dr. Morelle reflected how pleasant it would be to be in that train, roaring through the night, arriving at some quiet little West of England place, lost among the moors or snuggled down by the sea as dawn came up across the sky.

He sighed gently. Too much work ahead of him, here in London to dream long of a holiday such as he had briefly envisaged. The Harrow Road lay before him. A frown of distaste flicked across his aquiline features. This was an unsalubrious area of London; he felt an unreasonable twinge of irritation with Miss Frayle for bringing him into it.

A last minute change in his Scandinavian itinerary due to circumstances over which he'd had no control had brought him back to Copenhagen a week before he had anticipated. His hosts and their friends had tried hard to prevail upon him to take time out and spend the week in relaxation, but Dr. Morelle had not been persuaded. There was so much waiting to be done in London; he wanted to get back to his study and laboratory at 221b Harley Street.

He had accordingly had a cable sent earlier in the day to Miss Frayle, informing her of the time of his return and had expected her to be at London Airport to meet him, with chauffeur and hired car in attendance. To his astonishment there had been no sign of the familiar, fluttering figure. He had waited, dragging at his inevitable Le Sphinx in impatience until it had become apparent that Miss Frayle was not going to appear. His face set grimly, he had obtained a car to drive him to Harley Street, which he had reached just after half past six in the evening.

Here, too, he suffered a minor shock. For the usually ubiquitous Miss Frayle was for once nowhere in evidence. The study was impeccably tidy, his papers as neatly filed and docketed as ever, an accumulated mass of correspondence awaited him on his desk. It was then that the sight of the unopened cable among some other mail on the front doormat caused him to realize what must have happened. Whoever had been responsible for cabling Miss Frayle of his unexpectedly earlier return had obviously forgotten his instructions. She was to be reached not at Harley Street, but at Radio House, where she was undertaking the temporary assignment during his absence, as arranged by himself before he had left London.

Picking up the telephone in his study he had got on to Radio House, and the switchboard-operator put him through at once to someone whom she said might be able to give him the information he wanted. After a moment a man's voice said: 'Duty Office. Can I help you?' The man was suitably impressed when he realized who it was speaking and promptly set about obtaining the information Dr. Morelle sought regarding the whereabouts of Miss Frayle.

He was back shortly with the news that those working on the programme with which Miss Frayle was associated all appeared to have left the building, the man adding that it seemed most of those concerned had gone on to a party, and he was able to supply Dr. Morelle with the address where it was taking place.

Dr. Morelle was not particularly interested in hearing all this, it didn't sound very much like Miss Frayle. The sort of party he envisaged of broadcasting and literary people, actors and actresses did not sound at all the sort of setting he would expect her to blend into.

'In Blomfield Road, you know, Little Venice, by the canal,' the man said. Dr. Morelle said he knew, a little impatiently, and took the address. 'Perhaps you'd like to ring there and find out,' the man said. 'I can give you the number.'

But Dr. Morelle had replaced the receiver. Miss Frayle at a party, he mused, at a flat in Little Venice. A glint of frosty humour appeared in his eyes, and ten minutes later he was heading along Wigmore Street in the Duesenberg.

Now it was that heart-searching hour when night and day met, usurped each other's places, at the hour of the evening when London seemed magical. Lights gleaming, neon glowing, the sounds of traffic, voices blended into a soft murmur. Dr. Morelle had driven slowly, the hood of the car was down as he almost invariably preferred it, unless the weather was altogether too inclement, absorbing as much as he could of the mystery of the night. He had chosen to turn into the whirlpool of traffic spinning round

Marble Arch, before proceeding along the edge of Hyde Park, where the breeze sighed in the trees. Then, at Queensway, he had turned right and began to head towards Paddington and Maida Hill.

Now, the Harrow Road lay behind him, the road climbed uphill now. Delamere Road, it was, rising till it topped the canal. As the dark expanse of water came into sight, Dr. Morelle braked. There was no traffic, at this moment of the late evening, only a few strollers.

He stopped the car and he sat there, his face shadowed beneath the brim of his hat, his hands resting lightly on the steering wheel. He felt an urge to get out of the car and spend a few moments staring down at the gleaming water. He began to look for a place to leave the Duesenberg.

He turned left, over the bridge, and a few yards along saw the entrance to a narrow little street. Delicately he swung the Duesenberg into the turning. Warwick Place, he read. There was a public house, the Warwick Castle, and on the other side, a small café. A few silent shops, the back entrance to some tall houses, a yard. This was Warwick Place.

Dr. Morelle pulled the car into the kerb outside the Warwick Castle. He got out and walked slowly back to the canal. His footsteps echoed in the narrow alley, flanked by a brick wall on one side. Then he was in the wider sweep of Blomfield Road. He followed it round, and crossed to where he had nosed the car over the bridge.

He stood there, staring through the iron railings at the water. The canal widened here into a dark lake. To the left was a small public garden, neat with lawns and flower-beds, and the bridge that carried Warwick Avenue over the canal. Here, the water was starred with lights, street lights, lights from the tall houses on the other side of the canal. The island in the centre of the lake was dark and still but Dr. Morelle thought he saw the spectral gleam of a swan's feathers among the dark grass.

He took a cigarette from a thin gold cigarette-case and lit it, the flame of his lighter illuminating his lean face, the dark heavy brows over the long hooded eyes, the curving nose above the strong mouth and forceful chin. He allowed his thoughts to drift along in a reverie.

This was Little Venice and his mind went back to the Venice of the North, Stockholm, there where rock hills sloped to the salt waters of the Baltic inlet, Saltsjon and the brackish waters of great Lake Malaren. The city of islands and rocks which thrust upward above the level of the tides.

He was remembering the green of the trees and the lawns of the city, the brilliant flowers and the bright awnings of the cafés which contrasted so vividly with the old, grey buildings in the medieval, where the narrow houses huddled together beneath the serrated ranks of chimneys above the roofs, and everywhere in sight ships' masts and funnels clustered, beneath the sun, thick about the burnished waters of the inlets and coves.

His thoughts went back to one waning twilight when in company with two police-detectives he had hurried out of the building of the Statens Kriminalte-kniska Anstalt, which owed much to the great work of the late Harry Soderman, who had died only a little while ago in Tangier. In a police-car he had raced through the streets of Stockholm, the headlights had cut a great yellow wedge on the black macadam and the tyres had shrieked as the driver took the curves at speed.

That was the night when the body of a little girl had been found in the woods along a dirt road outside the city. Dr. Morelle was remembering the lanterns and flashlights as the police-car arrived, the uniformed policemen, the local precinct detectives and the mob of onlookers kept back from the scene. The floodlights bursting out, so that it was like day, more cars arriving to add their headlights to the brilliance, and the black ambulance from the city morgue, and police-squad cars. The photographers with their cameras, the footprint and fingerprint men laying out their kits.

And the little girl under a clump of bushes sprawled loosely on the ground, pale gold hair spreading out from under the little white cap she was wearing. And his own remark to the detective beside him that the child had obviously been dumped there after she'd been murdered. It had brought a glimmer of admiration in the other's eyes. It was the first lead which was to result in the apprehension, two days later, of the murderer.

Dr. Morelle had made use of the grim incident in a talk he had given next day to Stockholm's leading medical and legal minds, criminologists and sociologists, crime-reporters and editors, who had crowded the lecture-hall, to point up that murder is at any time, anywhere, a revolting business, and that the police investigator, the first official on the scene of the crime bears the first impact of the unpleasantness.

Even more than the pathologist who makes the autopsy, or the reporters covering the story, Dr. Morelle said, the unfortunate policeman is spared none of the details; from the moment the telephone rings in his office until the murderer is behind bars, he endures intense and sordid physical and psychological pressure. He must examine the victim with his own hands, without avoiding any detail, he must encounter those physical details including blood and vomit, the stench of decaying flesh, and even more repulsive matters.

Dr. Morelle had brought his talk to a close by reminding his audience of the more human aspects of murder, from the policeman's point of view. Children left fatherless; a mother loses her only son. The detective hears the tears and the despair of the mourner. The murderer is caught and a second tragedy is added to the first, the murderer like his victim is no less a human being.

Dr. Morelle's ruminations were interrupted by the metallic clatter of railway-trucks from the goods yard outside Paddington Station; nearer sounded a sudden raucous burst of drunken laughter from one of the mean streets across the water.

The spell broken, Dr. Morelle moved slowly round the curve of the road, crossed Warwick Avenue, looking down it to the tall structure of the ventilator shaft at Warwick Avenue Underground station, then he was in the wide quiet stretch of Blomfield Road that flanked the canal, running straight up to the Edgware Road.

Each house in the shadows was different in style and character, some simple, elegant, Georgian, others more ornate, flaunted their Victorian origins plainly. Dr. Morelle found the house he was seeking soon enough. Set back a little, fronted by flower-beds which by day must have been brilliant with dahlias and chrysanthemums, it gleamed whitely in the light from the street-lamps. Dr. Morelle crossed from the canal side, opened the front gate and heard voices through the open ground-floor windows.

He stood listening, with a slightly raised eyebrow. Someone sobbing, someone nearly hysterical. He went to the front door and rang the bell. There was a murmuring of voices from inside the hall. Doctor Morelle waited, pressed on the bell again. He heard it shrilling inside the house, and after a moment approaching

78

footsteps. The front door was jerked open.

'Are you the police — ?'

The voice broke off with a gasp of incredulous amazement as the familiar figure stared at him, her eyes huge behind their horn-rims.

'Good evening, Miss Frayle,' he said.

'Dr. Morelle,' she said with a gulp. 'I — I didn't know you were back — '

'You were expecting the police instead, it seemed?'

'Oh, Dr. Morelle,' she said, 'thank goodness you've come. A dreadful thing's happened. Someone's been murdered.'

7

It had been after Miss Frayle and Guy Keaping had left the balcony. They had exchanged only a few more words, Miss Frayle feeling convinced that she had said too much already, and then Guy Keaping had said it was time for him to be moving, he had an early meeting with a writer next morning.

It seemed to Miss Frayle that the sympathy which she had thought had existed between them during the past few weeks had suddenly evaporated. They were polite strangers. In the hall he had gone to find Blackwood to say goodnight, Miss Frayle returning to where the others were dancing. Raoul Dassinget's current partner had been Betty Lewis. They were locked together and she was looking up into his face, her own plain features alive and glowing.

'What a silly girl she is,' Miss Frayle had reflected, then the record stopped, the girl had frowned anxiously, Dassinget had glanced at his watch, and they had both hurried from the room. At that moment Bill Scott had appeared to ask if anyone had seen Carla. 'Probably being sick,' someone had suggested. Doug Blackwood had come in.

'If you're worried,' he said to Scott, 'better start a search. Only don't expect me to join in.' Raoul Dassinget had appeared, Miss Frayle couldn't help noticing the lipstick on his face, and Blackwood said to him: 'You'd better wipe your face.'

The other's grin was forced, as he felt in his pocket with what was meant to be bravado.

'Lost your handkerchief?' Bill Scott had said contemptuously, and he'd thrown his folded handkerchief at the Frenchman and turned and walked from the room.

'Play a record, can't someone?' Blackwood said to the group of people by the radiogram. 'Come on, Miss Frayle. Let's dance. At least you're not likely to throw your temperament around.'

Warm, languorous South American

music filled the room, and Miss Frayle had let the rhythm take over, she didn't want to talk, nor, it seemed, did Blackwood. He had danced expertly, but he was staring over her head, grimly, watchfully. And then Bill Scott had burst in. He was deathly white.

'Carla, she's dead. Oh, Christ, she's dead.'

The dancing stopped abruptly, only the music had gone smoothly on, until someone switched it off. Miss Frayle followed Blackwood over to Bill Scott. 'In the water,' he was saying incoherently. 'Someone's pushed her into the water.'

Miss Frayle had shot off after Blackwood through to the back of the house where an open door led down three steps and into the long garden. She heard the others hurrying after her. The sky was bright with stars, the trees in the garden twinkled with fairy lights. Blackwood ran down the path. In the soft light he looked immensely big and powerful and his hair was black as a crow's wing.

Half-way the garden dropped again to a lower level. There was a stone terrace and below it a postage-stamp of lawn with a large pond that was fed by the canal, running into the garden through a tunnel under a little footbridge. Everyone stopped at the top of the stone steps that led down to the water. Miss Frayle hesitated and watched the man before her jump clean down the steps and go to where Carla lay, sprawled face down, her red dress rucked up about her knees, her nylon seams twisted. Her right arm was flung out, the other under her body. Her head lolled over the edge of the pond and her hair floated out on the water.

Miss Frayle stood aside as Guy Keaping pushed past her down the steps after Blackwood. Together the two men dragged Carla away from the edge. Miss Frayle saw her face. It wasn't pretty any more. What was left of her makeup was in smears and streaks. 'She's dead all right,' she heard Blackwood say.

Someone else rushed past Miss Frayle and down the steps. It was Raoul Dassinget. His face looked green but it might have been the lights. Blackwood tried to hold him off but the Frenchman thrust him away. 'Carla,' he said hoarsely. Suddenly he put his head down on the sodden red frock. He pressed his face against the wet body, made as if to put his arms round it. Then he caught the gleam of an evening sandal which lay a little way off. He stumbled to it and picked it up. 'The heel is loose,' he said. 'She must have slipped. Slipped on the steps and fallen.'

Miss Frayle, hearing him, frowned. The water was too far away from the steps. Even if Carla Collins had fallen heavily she couldn't have rolled right to the pond, over the edge until her head was in the water. Miss Frayle saw Guy Keaping put out his hand towards the body, but Blackwood knocked it away. 'She mustn't be touched again until the police have seen her.'

'What's it in her hand?' Miss Frayle heard Keaping say.

'A handkerchief.' Doug Blackwood had looked grimly round. 'Looks like a man's. Anybody lost one to-night?'

Miss Frayle saw Dassinget wince. 'It could be mine,' he said slowly. 'I lent her a handkerchief earlier this evening. May I have it back please?'

'The police will return it to you,' Blackwood had stared at him and Miss Frayle moved to Blackwood.

'I'll ring them if you like,' she said.

He'd nodded and she'd turned back to the house. Suddenly a bony arm reached out of the darkness and gripped her wrist. It had been Bill Scott, his eyes glazed, he was trembling. 'Miss Frayle, it wasn't an accident. She was murdered. And I know who did it.'

She had decided he was hysterical and shaking off his grip, had dashed off to the telephone. And a few moments afterwards, the door-bell had rung and now here she was, staring at Dr. Morelle. Of all people. And she had imagined he was miles away in Oslo or Stockholm. Or was it Copenhagen?

Miss Frayle pulled herself together, took a grip on her confused mind, calmed her voice, steadied her fluttering hands. 'I'd telephoned the police,' she said. 'When you rang I thought it was them — ' She broke off helplessly. 'Do you mean to say you didn't know?'

'I came here to find you,' Dr. Morelle said acidly. 'To inquire why you had failed to look in at Harley Street today, where you would have found the cable asking you to meet the plane.'

Whatever answer that might have leapt to her tongue she was saved making it. Through the open front door behind Dr. Morelle two figures appeared. One of them gave an exclamation when he saw Dr. Morelle.

'Hello, Dr. Morelle? Fancy meeting you.'

It was Detective-Inspector Hood, the inevitable pipe stuck between his teeth, bowler hat in hand, with him a plain-clothes detective-sergeant. As the man from Scotland Yard spoke, Miss Frayle stepped forward and caught his eye. 'And Miss Frayle, too?' he said.

'It was I who phoned, Inspector Hood,' she said. 'Though I didn't know it would be you.'

The burly figure smiled at her easily from under his grey moustache. 'Which makes me all the more glad I happened to be around when the call came through to the Yard,' he said. He glanced at Dr. Morelle. 'Quite like old times, eh?'

At that moment Doug Blackwood appeared. He spoke quickly and calmly to Inspector Hood. Miss Frayle moved to Dr. Morelle, who had turned aside so that his back was to the others, and gave him a low-voiced explanation of what had transpired.

Blackwood had led Inspector Hood and the detective-sergeant towards the huddle of guests. Inspector Hood stared round at them. 'No one is to leave,' he said. He turned to the plain-clothes man beside him. 'If you'll get their names and addresses.' He padded off with Blackwood.

Over Dr. Morelle's shoulder, as she talked to him, Miss Frayle glimpsed Guy Keaping, standing by himself. She saw him shiver, find a cigarette and light it. Raoul Dassinget sat like some angular piece of sculpture, his eyes glassy. Only a muscle twitched in his cheek.

Miss Frayle swung round to the street as another police-car pulled up, joining the one which had brought Inspector Hood. Her experienced eyes recognized a police-surgeon, and photographers. They came up the path, marched into the house, took a quick look about them, and then, as though pulled by an invisible magnet, disappeared towards the garden.

Miss Frayle gave a nervous smile as she glanced at Dr. Morelle. 'You couldn't have turned up at a more opportune moment.'

'My dear Miss Frayle,' he said coldly, 'this is for the police to handle.'

He moved away swiftly and Miss Frayle watched him speak to the detective-sergeant, engaged in jotting down the names and addresses of those present. The man nodded, grinned affably at him and Dr. Morelle came back to Miss Frayle. 'In fact,' he said, 'I am on my way back to Harley Street. Perhaps you will return as soon as you can.'

And without another word he was striding swiftly down the path into Blomfield Road.

Miss Frayle stared after him in mingled surprise and dismay. He was obviously furious because she had not met him off his plane, and because he thought she was having fun at some party, instead of sitting waiting for him in the study beside his writing-desk. Although she knew he was behaving utterly unreasonably, it wasn't her fault that she hadn't received the news of his return earlier than had been planned, she felt a dim sense of guilt. It was infuriating to be made to feel that she was in the wrong.

She gave a heartfelt sigh and went into the room where the detective-sergeant was finishing his note-taking. He looked up at her, then his gaze wandered round the red and black furnishings and walls, fastened on the picture of the nude with the guitar, drifted back to her impassively and then bent over his note-book once more.

Miss Frayle found a chair next to Guy Keaping. She looked round at the dismal remnants of a party scattered about the room On one table a glass had been overturned and its contents dripped on to the carpet. She longed to go across and right it, but she could not have moved.

The very room was under a spell.

Inspector Hood came back into the room, his face giving nothing away, with Blackwood. Miss Frayle knew a sudden sympathy for Doug Blackwood. How frightful for this to have happened here. Had Carla Collins been murdered, as Bill Scott said? Who had done it? Miss Frayle glanced about her. One of the people in this very room, she thought, with a shudder.

Whoever it was could have held the wretched girl's head under water until she was dead, she had been too drunk to resist much. And then? Wrenched off one of her shoes, to suggest she had stumbled on the steps and fallen backwards into the water? Inspector Hood's voice broke into her musing.

'So I must please ask you all to remain here for a time. You understand I have to know something about the movements of the young woman. In the first place, those of you who spoke to her to-night, or danced with her, would you come forward please?'

There was a stir. Miss Frayle searched

her memory. Had she spoken to Carla? In any case she certainly knew one or two things that might interest Inspector Hood. She stepped forward with the others. Inspector Hood threw her a little smile then he turned to Doug Blackwood questioningly, who led him out to another room. Somewhere a clock chimed. Keaping who had stepped forward when she had, sighed gently and she looked at him. 'I expect this is all routine stuff for you?' he said.

'I don't know,' she said slowly. 'I've never before been on this side of the fence.'

'I suppose the girl fell down the steps and into the pond,' he said.

Did he really believe that? With a prickle of alarm she remembered Bill Scott pouncing on her in the darkness on her way to phonc the police, his harsh words in her ear. 'It wasn't an accident. She was murdered. And I know who did it.'

She looked for Scott now, and saw him huddled in a chair near where a uniformed policeman from the local police-station stood impassively. He had crumpled up, his pallor was ghastly. She saw the detective-sergeant come in and whisper to him. He went out of the room as though he was sleep-walking.

He was gone about ten minutes; during that time Guy Keaping got through another cigarette, Maria Fox made up her pretty, doll-like face as calmly as if she was in her own dressing-room; and Miss Frayle wondered nervously about Dr. Morelle impatiently waiting for her at Harley Street.

Then it was Raoul Dassinget's turn. He frowned, his mouth twitched a little, then he followed the plain-clothes man from the room with a travesty of his old swagger.

Someone went to the kitchen and made coffee. Miss Frayle took hers black and shuddered over it. The procession went on, Maria Fox; a couple of young men who'd danced with the dead girl; Miss Frayle was left till last. Guy Keaping went before her, sauntering off as casually as he could look. Miss Frayle decided he really didn't take it seriously.

When she went into the room, she found Inspector Hood behind a table, his bowler hat on a chair beside him. The detective-sergeant stood unobtrusively in the background. Inspector Hood apologized for making her wait so long, and when she couldn't resist saying that Dr. Morelle was expecting her at Harley Street, his smile faded and he muttered to himself. He referred to a sheet of paper in front of him. It looked like a time-table, with times down the left-hand margin and names across the top.

'I'll make it fast,' he said. 'Perhaps you could put me in the picture about the girl? I've been hearing some pretty different views. Seems a lot of people weren't exactly fond of her.'

'I didn't know her very well. She was a bit obvious, over made-up, always got her eye on the men.' Miss Frayle felt she sounded prudish, but she didn't know how best to describe the girl truthfully.

Inspector Hood asked her what she knew about Carla Collins and Raoul Dassinget. Miss Frayle told him about the scene that evening at Radio House, and about the row during the party in which Carla, Maria Fox and Dassinget had been concerned.

'What did you think of the Frenchman's heavy dramatics over the poor girl's body?'

'I thought he was sincere,' she said. 'A bit overdone, but after all, he's a Frenchman.'

The Scotland Yard detective nodded. 'When did you last see her?' he said.

'When she had the row with him. She'd obviously had too much to drink. Then the man Scott took her off somewhere. The next thing was when he rushed in and asked if anybody had seen her.' She recalled the scene with Keaping on the balcony overlooking the road, with the canal gleaming beyond. The time signal over the radio. Eleven o'clock. 'A minute or two later,' she said. 'Guy Keaping and I came downstairs.' Inspector Hood was writing on his timetable, and she said: 'What time was she — was she — ?' She broke off as he eyed her.

'About that time.'

While she was upstairs, then, with Guy

Keaping, Miss Frayle thought and felt glad for some reason.

'How long after Scott started looking for her before he rushed in and said she was dead?'

'I was dancing with Doug Blackwood,' Miss Frayle said slowly. 'Then Bill Scott rushed in.'

The door opened and the police-photographer put his head in. 'We've finished with her.' Inspector Hood nodded, the other nodded back and disappeared. The burly man at the table looked at Miss Frayle again.

'What do you know about this chap, Scott?'

Miss Frayle told him about the incident in the bar at Radio House. Bill Scott vowing he'd get his own back on Dassinget. She wondered if Bill Scott had told Inspector Hood what he'd told her when she'd rushed in to phone. She hesitated. He may have been talking wildly, she didn't want to involve him more if he hadn't meant what he'd said to her. All the same she'd better tell Inspector Hood all she knew. It was for him to decide what value it was. 'When I was rushing back to the house to phone, he grabbed me. He said her death was no accident. It was murder and he knew who'd done it.'

Inspector Hood nodded, without conveying whether he'd already learned this from Bill Scott himself, or not. Instead he asked her about Betty Lewis, and she told him that so far as she knew that young woman had left as soon as she'd finished dancing with Dassinget. She'd had a train to catch, Miss Frayle thought.

'She and the Frenchman,' Inspector Hood muttered broodingly, 'good friends?'

Miss Frayle said she wasn't so sure about that, though she remembered how Dassinget had held Betty Lewis close while they'd danced together, and how the girl had gazed up at him.

Then, Inspector Hood was thanking her for all her help, and asked her to convey his regrets to Dr. Morelle for making her so late. It wasn't until after she'd quit the room, that it occurred to Miss Frayle that if it was murder, and she was even more certain from Inspector

Hood's demeanour that it was, then Betty Lewis could be in a position to supply Raoul Dassinget with an alibi.

An alibi without which, it seemed to her, Raoul Dassinget could be in rather a tough spot.

8

Miss Frayle fitted her latchkey into the
front door, opened it gently and tiptoed
inside. The house was very quiet. There
was a ticking of a clock from the room
just inside the door. Miss Frayle knew she
was in for an awkward encounter with Dr.
Morelle. He had not been in a good
mood when he left the house in Blomfield
Road, requesting her to get back to
Harley Street as quickly as she could, and
now it was impossibly late. Perhaps he
hadn't waited up for her. Perhaps he
would leave it until tomorrow. Feeling
slightly more confident she made her way
to Dr. Morelle's study.

Then to her dismay she heard that
familiar cold voice, he had heard her
come in. She went into the study, where
he was seated behind the big desk. A
desk-lamp cast a pool of light upon the
papers he had been studying. His face
was shadowed, but she could see the grim

line of his mouth, the hooded eyes.

Her earlier confidence, her self-assurance with which she had bolstered herself up during the past few weeks while he had been away, was already melting. She was as much in awe of him as ever, as vulnerable as she had been before to his caustic tongue. Yet she was, after all, an efficient, sometimes she was tempted to believe an invaluable, secretary. Dr. Morelle was her employer, nothing more.

Deliberately, she made no reference to Carla Collins' death, she began to acquaint him with the various items of interest which had mounted up daily while he had been abroad. She indicated the notes she'd made in his diaries, the appointments she had fixed for him, correspondence she had answered on his behalf.

He made no comment, offered no word of thanks for all that she had done while at the same time she had been engaged on her job at Radio House. He gave a brief explanation of the reason for his return to London earlier than had been expected. He waited politely, she thought, for her to offer an apology for failing to meet him at the airport, and she as pointedly, she hoped, refused to oblige. Why should she? It wasn't her fault if his blessed cable hadn't reached her.

When she had brought him up to date with the notes and appointments, Dr. Morelle leaned back in his chair. 'May we know,' he said, 'how you have been enjoying your spell in the world of radio? I assume it has not been entirely confined to party-going and sudden death?'

She eyed him uncomfortably, she hated the way he could appear perfectly serious while all the time he knew she knew that he was laughing at her. 'It's been very interesting,' she said guardedly. 'I have been working on the Crippen case to-day.' He gave her an encouraging nod. 'I had no idea how fascinating radio can be. All the mechanics of it, the technicalities. I'd no idea of the amount of work that goes on behind a programme.'

'I am gratified to learn that you feel your fund of knowledge has been increased,' he said drily. 'You will, of course, be returning to my employ. There is a mass of work arising out of my Scandinavian tour, which I'm sure you will find fascinating also.'

She stared at him with dismay. 'You mean leave there right away?'

'It was understood that you were there on a temporary basis. Unless you have any particular reason for wishing to remain longer?'

She blushed, stammered. 'I suppose not. But they were expecting me to help them with the next programme. The Vaquier case.'

'In which event,' he said, 'it seems they, whoever they may be, have a disappointment in store.'

She caught the unmistakable acid note in his voice and hastily she went off at a tangent. 'You know I'm sure that wretched girl was murdered. I mean I don't see how she could have fallen into the water like that.'

'And no doubt you passed on your conclusions to Inspector Hood,' he said coldly, and bent over the papers on his desk once more. He didn't glance up even when the telephone shrilled. She picked up the receiver. It was a man's voice at the other end. For a moment she failed to recognize it. She supposed she was expecting that it might be a call from Inspector Hood. When she realized it was Guy Keaping her heart leapt.

'Hello?' she said a little breathlessly.

At the other end of the line he sounded guarded. 'I've just got away.' Miss Frayle had glimpsed him in the hall as she'd hurried out from the house after leaving Inspector Hood, and had wondered vaguely why he hadn't gone like the others. 'Thought you might like to know,' he was saying, 'that they tried to get hold of Betty Lewis.'

'Oh, yes.'

'But when they phoned her home she hadn't arrived. It seemed she'd probably missed the last train.'

The question flashed through her mind, why had he taken the trouble to phone her and tell her this? If Betty Lewis had rushed away from the party too late, and missed her train, what of it? She remembered how the girl had looked at

Raoul Dassinget's watch and then run for it. She had been dancing with Doug Blackwood, she recalled. After she and Guy Keaping had come downstairs and he had left her rather abruptly. 'It's very kind of you to phone me,' she said uncertainly.

'Only why?' he said. 'Was that what you were going to say?'

'No, of course, I'm very interested.'

'That's what I thought,' he said, and she caught the mocking note in his voice. And then he sounded far away and remote.

'Good night,' she said and hung up. She glanced at Dr. Morelle who appeared absorbed in what he was reading. She longed to ask him what he thought of the grim tragedy which had struck so suddenly at the house in Little Venice, Guy Keaping telephoning her like this, and a dozen other questions that were spinning round in her head. 'Is there anything further?' she said.

'Good night, Miss Frayle,' he said, still bent over the desk. 'I will see you to-morrow.' His hair, in the soft glow of the desk-lamp was raven black, save where grey touched the temples. His high forehead was uncreased. His hooded eyes were fixed on the notes he was studying. His mouth was a tight grim line. Miss Frayle sighed, and went quietly out of the study.

She climbed the stairs to her top-floor flat and closed the door behind her. She was pretty weary. It had been a long day, her mind went over and over the incidents of the evening. The quarrels, the final horror. Somewhere in that whole chaotic evening there must be something that pointed to the explanation of the mystery surrounding Carla Collins' death.

Miss Frayle brushed her hair, took off her horn-rimmed spectacles and placed them carefully on her bedside table. Then in pyjamas and dressing-gown she sat on the edge of her bed and brooded on the party. Somewhere in the house a clock chimed midnight. She heard Dr. Morelle's foot-steps downstairs, the slam of a door.

Then the house was silent, with the

breathing silence of a house that is lived in. Miss Frayle had begun to walk restlessly about the room. The more she thought about the party, the more confused she became. Faces whirled through her mind. Carla Collins, outrageously provocative in that red low-cut dress; Guy Keaping drinking with the quiet desperation of a man with something on his mind; Doug Blackwood, strong and calm as his party became a shambles; young Bill Scott hysterical and bitter, Betty Lewis dancing with Raoul Dassinget and gazing into his eyes. Dassinget himself, dark and gaunt, sure of himself, then later crazed with grief. Or was it fear?

She began to doubt if after all it had been anything else other than an accident. It seemed incredible that anyone would go so far as to murder someone like Carla Collins, for all that she was a bit of a hussy. Yet, Guy Keaping had obviously decided that there'd been something sinister about her death. After all, didn't that account for his phoning her about Betty Lewis? As if her whereabouts would prove to be important. As if, Miss Frayle wondered, he knew that the girl would help Raoul Dassinget with an alibi which could come in useful?

Miss Frayle's head began to swim, as one moment she felt certain it was murder, and the next she wasn't so sure, it seemed so utterly out of tune with the people who'd been there at the party.

Suddenly she stopped pacing her bedroom. An idea had occurred to her. She opened the door and listened. The house was quiet. On tiptoe she crept down the stairs, past the landing where Dr. Morelle's bedroom was, and on down to the study. Once inside she closed the study door. Dr. Morelle's presence was still strong in the room, the aroma of his Le Sphinx cigarette, the shaving lotion he used.

Once or twice she looked nervously over towards the desk, as if expecting to see him there, but the chair was empty. She went over to where the dictaphone apparatus stood. She had used it often enough. With urgent fingers she set up a new cylinder and started the machine. Then, in unconscious imitation of Dr. Morelle, she began. 'Account of some significant happenings at the party which took place at Doug Blackwood's house in Blomfield Road, the night of Friday, 26th September.'

Her voice was self-conscious and nervous at first, she could hear it. But as she continued it steadied, and the importance of what she was saying took over from the way she was saying it. 'I arrived about eight o'clock, some other people arrived about the same time, Guy Keaping for one. There seemed to be some hostility existing between him and Doug Blackwood. They didn't seem to like each other I thought. I danced with Bill Scott, who said he thought Carla Collins was hard done by.'

Miss Frayle paused in her pacing and gave a triumphant little smile to herself. This would help her to make up her mind about it. By talking it out this way, she could decide what poor Carla Collins' death did add up to.

'I danced with Raoul Dassinget,' she

said into the dictaphone. 'He warned me to be careful of Guy Keaping while we were dancing Keaping was watching us. Then I danced with Doug Blackwood. It was then that the first odd incident occurred.'

Miss Frayle drew a deep breath. Recalling Carla's drunkenness, her scene with Dassinget, was decidedly unpleasant. But she went through with it, searching her memory for the things Carla had said, Dassinget's bitter retorts, and Maria Fox's interruption. 'At the end of all this, Carla said a curious thing. At least it struck me that way. She turned to Guy Keaping, who'd been looking on at all this, and said for him to tell Dassinget he'd better see her, maybe he could understand then. Later when I asked Keaping what she had meant, he said I must have misunderstood what she was saying, and then he changed the subject.'

Miss Frayle suddenly realized how tired she was and abruptly she sat down on a chair. 'After that,' she said, 'Guy Keaping wanted to show me over the house,' she described the layout of the place. 'We went through on to the balcony overlooking the Regent's Park Canal, and talked for a while. It was then that I asked him what Carla had meant by appealing to him to talk to Dassinget about her, and he pretended I had misunderstood what she'd said. It was as if there was something to do with the three of them, Keaping and Dassinget and the girl. I heard the radio at eleven p.m. with the news summary. This came from Doug Blackwood's bedroom. I don't know if he was in the bedroom.'

She recalled thinking that perhaps Blackwood had followed her and Keaping to eavesdrop on them for some reason. 'Then Keaping and I went back downstairs. He said he was going home, and he went off to find Blackwood to say good night. At this time, that is to say a few minutes past eleven, I saw Raoul Dassinget dancing with Betty Lewis. When the music stopped she asked him the time. Then they both hurried off.'

Something at this point worried Miss Frayle. She saw the scene again in her mind's eye, Betty Lewis's question to

Dassinget, his glance at his watch, her rush from the room. As though she was afraid of missing the last train. Dassinget going with her. Her tired brain laboured over the point but could see no gleam of light.

'Just after this,' she went on slowly, 'Blackwood came in, then Bill Scott, he asking if anyone had seen Carla. Then Dassinget appeared, grinning, with a lipstick smear on his face. Blackwood said something about he'd better wipe his face. Dassinget felt for his handkerchief but his pocket was empty. Bill Scott threw him his. Dancing started again and I danced with Doug Blackwood He seemed preoccupied and hardly spoke. Then Scott, who'd gone off presumably to look for Carla, rushed in and said he'd found her dead.'

Miss Frayle was drooping now. She forced herself up from the chair and began to pace about again, and described the scene as she had seen it when Carla's body was found by the others. The rush out into the garden, down the path, the shimmer of the fairy-lamps, the sprawled body by the pond, the head over the edge. One shoe, some distance away.

She described how Dassinget had flung himself on the body, how Carla had held a man's handkerchief gripped in her fingers, and Dassinget saying the handkerchief was his, that he had lent her one earlier in the evening; and how hurrying back to the house to telephone for the police, Bill Scott had told her he knew who'd murdered Carla.

She was nearing the end now and she quickened her speed. Dr. Morelle's arrival at the house. Inspector Hood and the rest of it. 'Then,' she said, 'Guy Keaping phoning me about Betty Lewis missing her train.'

At last she had finished. Wearily she switched off the dictaphone and stood tottering with fatigue.

She was so nearly asleep she barely heard the door open. Dr. Morelle came quietly into the room. 'If you've quite finished, Miss Frayle,' he said smoothly, 'I think you should go to bed, you really cannot expect to be fresh for work in the morning.'

9

She had overslept. When at last she struggled slowly to consciousness and looked at her bedside clock she saw with horror that it was a quarter past nine. She flung the bed-clothes off. Hastily she bathed, scrambled into her clothes, brushed her hair. Agitatedly she grabbed her horn-rimmed spectacles. There was no time even for a cup of tea. Dr. Morelle would be waiting for her downstairs.

She burst into the study. He was not there. Propped up on his desk was a note, in his meticulous handwriting. With a sinking heart Miss Frayle picked it up, then sighed with relief. It was not a rebuke. Not a piece of his sarcasm. 'I have to call upon Sir Hiram Peel, to discuss some data I brought back with me. I shall return after lunch. Perhaps you would start on the first folder.'

A large grey folder had been conspicuously placed in the centre of the desk. It was full of papers, all in that neat handwriting. It looked like a week's work. She crossed to the window and stood staring out across Harley Street. A row of gleaming cars stood in the front of the tall dignified houses. There was an air of assured opulence about the street. Nothing violent could happen here. Nothing sordid or dangerous.

At the southern end of Harley Street lay Cavendish Square. Miss Frayle closed her eyes and pictured the trees, lofty, their leaves brown and gold. There would be dead leaves drifting down to be crunched underfoot. These last few days of September were crisp and golden. London was at its most attractive, no longer hot and dusty as it had been in August, but relaxed, warm, benevolent. She could see in her mind's eye the flimsy summer dresses that had vanished from the windows of the great stores, in their place the elegant wax models were cosily warm in tweed suits, autumn-coloured coats. On the busy street the brisk shoppers and the noisy impatience of cars and taxis would add a sparkle to the day.

An idea occurred to her. She pushed Dr. Morelle's note into her pocket, and was out of the study and upstairs to fetch her handbag and coat. A minute or two later her shoes were tapping on the sunny pavement down Harley Street. Dr. Morelle had made no comment in his note about her giving up her job at Radio House. All he thought she had to do, no doubt, was just pick up the phone and tell someone they'd had it, Dr. Morelle was back and needed her.

In a few minutes she was entering Cavendish Square. It was everything she had imagined, and she paused for a moment, staring up at the great trees framed against the sky. Then she took the little street that ran alongside the massive building of a popular store, and a moment later she was in the hurly-burly of Oxford Street.

She plunged into a strong current, to be carried into a tide of people, borne along with them, no longer a separate entity, but a fragment of a great swarming mass. She saw the bus-stop outside another big store, and wrenched herself out of the stream. A number 6 would take her the way she wanted to go, or a number 60, buses that turn right out of Oxford Street and lumber off down Regent Street to Piccadilly and the Haymarket.

It was a number 60 which came first. She stepped on to it and started up the stairs. She chose a seat on the left-hand side. She always sat on the left-hand side, she felt curiously piqued if she was forced to sit on the right. It was an irrational habit, she knew, and she had often wondered what Dr. Morelle would make of it, if ever she'd had the nerve to ask him.

She relaxed, travelling in London buses was like taking time out from living. There was the rest of humanity struggling on the pavements below, there was the unceasing strategic battle of the drivers of vehicles; but up there on the top of the bus, comfortable, warm, there was nothing to do but watch and wait for the arrival at the destination. The bus heaved itself ponderously round in the middle of Oxford Circus and turned into Regent Street.

This was a street Miss Frayle loved; its wide sweep, its harmonious architecture, its elegant shops, full of accoutrements of the wealthy. She gazed saucer-eyed at the rich oriental fabrics in one wide store-window, at the distinguished autumn fashions in another, while she gave herself over to a day-dream of herself dressed in wonderful clothes, leading the life of some leisured society girl. She came out of her reverie with a sigh as the bus rolled down towards Piccadilly Circus.

The tourist season was not over yet. She observed obvious Americans, the men in wide-brimmed hats, the women carrying slung bags on leather straps from their shoulders. Scandinavians, unmistakable with their blondness, their tallness, their unashamed tourist-ness. And hundreds, thousands of Londoners, hustling, jostling, scowling to themselves against the noise, the activity of Piccadilly Circus.

Down Haymarket, and no more big stores, but offices, the advertisements of steamship-lines, past Her Majesty's Theatre, and the columns of the Haymarket

Theatre, and round the corner into Pall Mall and along to Trafalgar Square, with its fountains and lion figures, its rubbernecks and street photographers, and into the Strand.

Since she had been working at Radio House, Miss Frayle had come to know every turning off the Strand. It was not, she thought, a very agreeable street. The Charing Cross end of it in particular had a raffish, rather cheap atmosphere that she did not like at all.

She recalled that Dr. Morelle had once told her that he found it entirely fascinating. To see it at its best, he'd said, it needed the murk of a November day, when fog was drifting up from the river. Then with all the shops brightly lighted, the jewellers' windows gleaming, the coffee-shops sending out a warm inviting smell, then, the Strand had a nostalgic quality that few other London streets could equal.

The bus was turning the corner into the Aldwych as she went downstairs. She jumped off before it had stopped, and jay-walked along the middle of the

Aldwych until she found an opportunity to cross. A few minutes later she was opening the door of Guy Keaping's office. The chair behind his desk was empty, she stood by her own chair, where she had spent so many hours discussing scripts with him, and put her hands on the back of it.

The door was flung open, startling her, and a girl clerk brought a memo in and laid it on the desk, smiling at her cheerfully. Miss Frayle went along to the canteen. She saw Guy Keaping at once, Betty Lewis was sitting with him, over coffee. Miss Frayle contemplated finding an empty table, but then he glanced up, saw her, and waved his hand in invitation.

Suddenly conscious that she had eaten no breakfast, Miss Frayle took two current buns and three dabs of butter. Trim and slim, she had no need to worry about her waist-line. Her statistics never varied, whether she ate salads or rich pastries. She collected a large cup of coffee, and made her way to Guy Keaping's table.

He looked at her quizzically. 'How's

Dr. Morelle today?'

Betty Lewis gave a sour laugh. 'Seems he arrived at quite an appropriate moment.'

'Hope he didn't mind my phoning you?' Keaping said.

'Not a bit,' Miss Frayle said, absently. She stared at the Lewis girl. How could she appear so callous? Betty Lewis read her thoughts and shrugged. 'Can't pretend I'm bursting with grief because she came to a sticky end. If anybody asked for it, she did.'

'Have you seen the papers?' Keaping said. 'They're fairly gone to town on it.'

Miss Frayle looked at him over the rim of her cup of coffee. She had glimpsed the newspaper headlines before she'd hurried from the house in Harley Street. She saw that Betty Lewis was watching her curiously. 'What theories has Dr. Morelle got? Or is a sordid business like that beneath his notice?'

Miss Frayle smiled at her. 'It's really rather ridiculous to think of him as some kind of amateur detective,' she said. 'He's nothing of the sort, he's a psychiatrist more than a criminologist.'

'All the same,' Betty Lewis said insistently, 'he has been mixed up in criminal investigations, I know, I read about him; and he did happen to turn up last night. Just after Carla Collins was done in.'

'But was she murdered?' Miss Frayle said. 'It isn't definite — '

'Don't kid yourself,' Betty Lewis said interrupting her. 'Someone took the chance of catching her when she was drunk and shoved her head in the pond. And held it there.'

Miss Frayle felt a little sick at the other's words and put down her coffee. She caught Guy Keaping's glance and she turned to Betty Lewis. Casually, buttering one of her currant-buns, she managed to say: 'Anyway, you missed being questioned by the police last night.'

'I know.'

'Must be a bore living out of town,' Keaping said. He threw Miss Frayle what she took to be a meaning glance. 'When you're out on a party. When is your last train?'

'Eleven-fifteen. I missed the damn thing last night, and had to stay with a friend.'

Suddenly Miss Frayle grasped the odd fact which had eluded her last night. Betty Lewis hadn't left the house until well after eleven o'clock, nearer ten minutes past, at a guess. Miss Frayle had left the balcony with Guy Keaping soon after eleven, she had seen the girl dancing with Dassinget then. 'You must have cut it pretty fine,' Miss Frayle said. 'It was after eleven o'clock when you dashed for it.'

The other looked at her sharply. 'It was ten minutes to when I told Raoul I had to go.' A complacent smile appeared on her plain features. 'He was rather peeved. He said he was just beginning to enjoy dancing with me.'

Miss Frayle told herself that she must try and get it clear. She had come downstairs with Guy Keaping — she glanced at him now, but he seemed to be absorbed in lighting a cigarette — a few minutes past eleven. As they got to the door of the room where people were dancing, she had seen the girl dancing with Dassinget. The dance ended. Betty Lewis looked as if she'd asked Dassinget the time, then they'd both hurried out. So how could it have been ten minutes before eleven?

'For heaven's sake, don't try to make a mystery out of it,' Betty Lewis said, snappily, and Miss Frayle realized the girl's eyes had been boring into her. 'Raoul's watch was slow or something.'

Miss Frayle said vaguely she expected that was what it was. 'The cops got hold of you this morning?' she heard Keaping say.

'They were here five minutes after I arrived,' Betty Lewis said. 'I'd read about it in the papers by then. It was a couple of plain-clothes men, very agreeable. I told them what I knew which wasn't much.'

Her eyes had become hard as pebbles, Miss Frayle thought, and she was smirking to herself as if she knew some secret, then she got up from the table, her head high, and went off. Miss Frayle wondered if her withdrawn expression had anything to do with Raoul Dassinget.

She was remembering the lipstick on the Frenchman's face when he came back into the room.

She looked at Guy Keaping, her eyes wide and innocent behind their horn-rims. 'I came to say good-bye,' she said. 'Dr. Morelle needs me.'

'I'm sure he does,' he said gently, holding her with his warm gaze. He drew at his cigarette. 'You must have found us poor company after him,' he said, and there was a trace of bitterness in his tone. 'We're second-raters, the lot of us here. People who weren't bright enough, or quick enough, to jump on to the television band-wagon. The also-rans, the old faithfuls of steam-radio.'

He exhaled a cloud of cigarette smoke, and she felt a pang of disappointment. Was this all he had to say now she was going? They had finished their coffee and by mutual consent they got up from the table and walked out of the canteen. They waited for the lift. He remained silent while it bore them up and he followed her to the door of the office and opened it for her.

Sun was streaming through the high windows, glinting on the chromium handles of the great green filing cabinets, gleaming on the noiseless typewriter she had typed his scripts on. The light oak furniture, the chairs with their green leather seats, the fawn-coloured carpet on the floor; all these things had become familiar to Miss Frayle.

Yet she was glad to be going now. A sinister element seemed to have taken possession of the place with that wretched girl's death, and she found herself filled with a sense of foreboding. Insecurity was in the air here, frustration and aggressiveness. And above all the conviction that someone in this very department had done Carla Collins to death. 'Why did you phone me last night about Betty Lewis?' she asked the heavy-featured man who was eyeing her.

He moved behind his desk and swivelled into the chair. 'That's what you asked before,' he said. 'And I told you. Because I thought you might be interested. After all, sudden death is your racket. Or your boss's.' He paused.

'Perhaps you wanted to know if she'd spent the night with Raoul Dassinget. How should I know? Some people think he's attractive.'

She blushed. Her eyes sparkled behind her horn-rims. 'I really don't think that kind of information would amuse me,' she said bitingly.

Immediately he realized that he'd said the wrong thing. 'I'm sorry, I shouldn't have said that. I was only trying to be funny. It's the sort of humour that appeals round here.' He came across to her. He put out his hands and took one of hers gently. 'You're lucky to be able to get away from this dump. And it isn't going to get any cosier here.'

She gulped. Suddenly she wanted to give him a kiss on his cheek, but she didn't do so. Instead she turned and was gone from the office.

The man stood quite still when she had gone, a curious expression on his face. Then, abruptly, he made as if to go after her. He got as far as the door but then he stopped. Why had he phoned her last night? He hadn't given a damn about the police chasing after Betty Lewis. He supposed, his face shadowing, he'd expected that she would throw him some sort of life-line for him to hang on to. Only he hadn't had the guts to call for help.

He shook his head and moved slowly back to the desk, his shoulders hunched. Sitting in the big swivel chair he pulled a folder towards him.

10

Well, Miss Frayle reflected, that hadn't got her very far. Though, come to think, was she altogether sure what she had been after? Her visit to Radio House had been a spur-of-the-moment notion. It was on the bus on which she was returning to Harley Street that she had a further idea, and at the bus-stop in Oxford Street she got off and hurried across Oxford Circus, to dive down into the musty and gusty tube-station to find a telephone.

On the way from Radio House she had been carefully ticking off the various items which ran round her head, while at the same time she had recalled the dictaphone-notes she had made last night. From what Betty Lewis said over coffee that morning it seemed to Miss Frayle that Raoul Dassinget had no alibi at the time of Carla Collins' death, which had occurred at approximately ten minutes to eleven.

Betty Lewis had made the point that she had been dancing with him, but in fact, they might not have begun dancing until a few minutes prior to eleven p.m. The girl had died a short while before then. So that he could have killed Carla Collins, and easily returned and danced with Betty Lewis. And then there was that odd business about the time by his watch. Might he not have deliberately misled her by several minutes? Enough to provide him with an alibi?

Betty Lewis missing her train, she thought, had some significance. She had realized, of course, the proper action for her to take. Tell Dr. Morelle. She had wondered if he'd listened to the stuff she'd dictated, and what he'd thought of it and she blushed at the prospect. He had made it clear to her that he had no intention of butting in on what was purely a police investigation. So whatever information she gave him, he would pass it on to Inspector Hood. If he thought it would be worth the trouble, that is.

And then this idea, and here she was in a telephone-box at Oxford Circus tube-station. She dialled Radio House, and encountered her first snag. Raoul Dassinget wasn't in his office, and further inquiry produced the information that he wasn't expected in to-day. She was about to hang up, defeated at the very start, when she thought to ask for his address. She said who she was, and after holding on while she was transferred first to this voice at the other end of the wire, then to another, she eventually learned that the Frenchman had a flat in a block in Grove End Road.

She scribbled down the address and hurried out of the call-box and out of the smell of the tube-station into the fresh, if noisy air of Oxford Circus. She crossed over and she waited for a bus.

Once again she was acting on impulse. She shouldn't be doing this, she should be back at Harley Street engrossed in work for Dr. Morelle. But the past weeks at Radio House had unsettled her, given her a feeling of independence. She had been listened to with respect by people like Doug Blackwood and Guy Keaping, and others working on the programme.

She had been made to feel important, as if she was quite an expert on criminology herself.

And then there had been Dr. Morelle's sudden return, his utter disinterest in Carla Collins' death; his calm manner of taking it for granted that Miss Frayle would be back in his study immediately, with hardly a word of good-bye to her Radio House job. It had all been most upsetting; she wanted to show people, Dr. Morelle, Guy Keaping, Doug Blackwood, Inspector Hood and the rest, that she did know a murderer when she met one.

A bus going up Baker Street and on up Park Road would take her somewhere near Grove End Road, but further than that she had not considered it. Only when she was on top of the bus and looking out across the September glory of Regent's Park, did she give some thought to the matter. By then it was too late. Her nearest point on this particular bus would be the corner of St. John's Wood Road.

She jumped off at the traffic lights. She swung left, down St. John's Wood Road, past the closed gates and high wall of

Lord's cricket ground, and turned right into Grove End Road. The block of flats, Grove Mansions, it was called, wasn't difficult to find. A great modern stream-lined block, glaringly white among its more sober neighbours. There was a wide drive-in for cars. Miss Frayle stood for a moment eyeing the place. It was all she disliked in this sort of thing, huge, glossy, impersonal, over-opulent.

She heard the taxi pull in to the kerb beside her, heard the slam of the door, then a familiar voice spoke in her ear and she spun round.

'Seems I'm just in time,' Guy Keaping said, smiling at her humorously.

'What on earth are you doing here?'

'One of those lucky coincidences,' he said lightly. 'I chanced to have looked in at address-index, it was an actor I wanted to get hold of, and I heard one of the girls giving Dassinget's address over the phone. It was for you. I hoped I'd be quick and get here in time to stop you.'

'Stop me from what?'

'What kind of idiot are you to go butting in on him, all on your little ownsome?' He spoke with a subdued violence, throwing the words at her as if they were stones. She could only stand there wide-eyed at him. 'Are you hoping to trap him into confessing he murdered Carla? How naïve can you get?'

Her voice trembled, he had come too close to the mark. 'If you must know,' she said carefully, trying to control her tone. 'I want to see him about something quite different.' She gave him what she hoped was a meaningful smile, inventing as hard as she could go. 'To tell you the truth, I have run across something in which he's deeply involved.' She sank her tone to a suitable whisper.

He made no reply, but stood looking at her, his brows contracted in a frown. Something told him that she was merely giving rein to her vivid imagination. Then, muttering to himself, he turned on his heel and walked away. She wondered if his intention was to try and get in touch with Dr. Morelle.

She hesitated, glanced at her wrist-watch. It was approaching one o'clock. She ought to be thinking about getting back to Harley Street, grabbing a sandwich *en route*, and getting on with the work in that folder. Then she tightened her jaw and she went across the drive-in and pushed through the big swing doors. This shouldn't take her many minutes, after all.

Inside she stopped and looked round the subdued, thickly carpeted hall. No one in sight, the porter's desk empty. Despite the bright sunshine outside, hidden wall-lamps were burning. There were two impossibly luxurious arm-chairs in an alcove. On one of the walls an obscure piece of surrealism hung in a rather nasty frame. The flat she wanted was on the third floor, where was the lift? She discovered it, faked up to look like part of the wall. There was a notice pinned on one of the doors. 'Lift Out of Action. Please Use Stairs.'

They were wide, shallow, carpeted stairs, with more wall-lamps burning at intervals. Whoever built this place, Miss Frayle ruminated, had been allergic to daylight. Perhaps, she reflected fancifully, it was too cheap a commodity for the opulent tenants. Toiling upwards, Miss Frayle felt the first pang of doubt. Was she doing a very foolish thing in coming here? What could she say to Dassinget, really? What reason could she give for her visit?

She turned a corner and went on up the next flight. Her heart was beginning to flutter. Suddenly she became aware of a small noise, a faint, regular squeak. Someone was coming up the stairs behind her.

She gasped and hurried on, her eardrums taut. It must be one of the tenants, forced to plod up the stairs as she was doing. On the next turn she paused for a moment; there it was again, the protest of shoes that not even the deep carpet could silence. The place was unnaturally quiet.

On the next landing she looked along the rather narrow, artificially lighted corridors. All the doors along them were shut. Faintly from one flat she heard music from a radio; once there was the slam of a door; but she saw no one. She went on up.

The squeak behind her was louder, but

the owner never came into view. Either a naturally slow walker, thought Miss Frayle nervously, or someone who was purposely keeping out of sight. She quickened her step, and came upon the third floor landing. The flats lay to her left; to her right was a turning, to a wall was pinned a notice with a pointing hand: 'Emergency Stairs.'

Flat 326, the one she wanted, must be at the far end of the corridor, she decided, looking at the number on the door nearest her. She started to look for it.

'Miss Frayle.' She wheeled round. Someone had called her. But there was no one in the corridor. She blinked, she was imagining things. She found flat 326 and was about to ring the bell. Then she heard the voice behind her again.

'Miss Frayle, can you come? I think I'm going to — ' The voice broke off, just as she had thought there was something familiar about it, though she couldn't quite place it. A groan and the voice tailed away. She stood listening. Nothing. No one. She turned away from the flat, went back along the corridor to the stair-head. No one on the stairs. Then again: 'By the stairs. I'm hurt.'

The other stairs, not these, she thought. She went along towards the emergency exit. She knew the voice now. She found herself at the emergency staircase. She realized two things. No luxury here. It ended abruptly with the carpet. The stairs were shadowy, bare, steep, twisting round a dark wall. No injured man here, needing help. But a movement behind her, someone in the shadows, someone with squeaking shoes.

She twisted round, panic-stricken. But she was too late. She heard an indrawn breath, felt a blow on the back of her head. She staggered, lost her balance, fell, and in falling crashed against the wall.

Her head filled with bright lights, then she lost consciousness.

11

Sir Hiram Peel's house was in Redington Road, in Hampstead. It was half-past twelve when Dr. Morelle emerged from the house, and came down the path towards the front gate, a distinguished figure in his impeccably cut dark grey, single-breasted suit. Crisp linen showed at his cuffs; his gloves were of the finest, softest chamois. He liked the feel of gloves when his hands were at the wheel of the car. He stepped across the pavement to where the long yellow Duesenberg was awaiting him.

The morning he thought perfect. Hampstead at its best on this early autumn day; the heath took on a mellowness it knew at no other time of year. Had he the time to drive along the heath? Dr. Morelle considered the matter. He had left Miss Frayle plenty of work. It was unlikely that she would require more for some hours to come. He felt the need for a breath of fresh air, after Sir Hiram's rather tedious dissertations. Why were legal men so often prosy? At their best they scintillated and gleamed like a well-cut diamond; at the other extreme they could heap verbosity upon verbosity.

The engine of the Duesenberg roared into life. Dr. Morelle drove slowly up Redington Road and turned right, at the top, into West Heath Road. Along the side of the heath, then he turned sharply left and went up towards North End Road. Here he paused for a moment, his foot on the brake, wondering whether to go on up the Spaniards or come down East Heath Road. He chose the latter, turned about and slid smoothly down East Heath Road, with the heath on his left.

The rolling grassland, dry and springy after a fair September, trees turning colour, brackeny woodland. He stopped the car, breathing deeply. He took off his hat, his sombre face was alight with pleasure, the mildest breeze stirred his dark, greying hair. He knew the woody glades of the heath pretty well, he mused, as he listened to the brown leaves crackling across the path.

There had been the murder of the old financier, whose body had been discovered one misty moonlight night a year ago sitting on a seat beside a path down in the Vale of Health. As a result of his investigation of certain aspects of the case, he had come to know the sudden drops and steep hillsides.

It would be pleasant, he thought, to proceed as far as Ken Wood, and spend a little time with the paintings in the Iveagh Collection; but there was so much sifting through of material he had brought back with him from his Scandinavian trip. The paintings of Gainsborough and Hals, of Rubens and Romney, Turner and Rembrandt must wait till another day.

The Duesenberg continued along East Heath Road, carried on down South End Road into Pond Street and Rosslyn Hill. His thoughts went before him and centred on Miss Frayle. Suggesting her to the Radio House people, that had been a mistake. She had tasted the heady waters of a somewhat irresponsible, not to say raffish way of earning a living, and it had obviously gone to her head.

It would require some time, he thought, before she regained the single-minded concentration he required of her. His reflections turned to the house in Little Venice and the death of the young woman. The incident, he thought rather epitomised the atmosphere and general circumstances of Miss Frayle's temporary employment. A wild party, too much liquor, emotions allowed to get out of hand, and a sordid tragedy. Accident or murder, it was not the sort of unpleasantness with which he considered a confidential secretary of his ought to be in the slightest way connected.

Scowling a little he sped down Haverstock Hill, turned right into Regent's Park Road, and turned into Prince Albert Road. He would like to have gone by way of the Outer Circle, enjoying the freshness of Regent's Park, but he kept to the road, driving fast, cleaving a way through buses and taxis. Park Road, Baker Street, Marylebone Road; now he was on familiar ground. A few minutes later he turned down Harley Street and pulled up outside his house.

He went into the study, Miss Frayle was not there. Frowning he looked in the laboratory, though there was no reason so far as he knew for her being there. The folder he had left her was all she required to carry on work. He called upstairs to her, but there was no reply. No message from her on his desk. He lit a cigarette irritably. Where on earth had she got to?

A glance at the folder indicated that she had not started on the job. A thought occurred to him and he crossed to the dictaphone. He recalled Miss Frayle's midnight visit to the study. He had intended to play the machine back to hear what she had dictated, now he wondered if she had left some message on the dictaphone for him this morning.

This might be some strange idea of efficiency she had evolved, or some eccentricity she had picked up during her work at Radio House. With a sigh of exasperation he began playing back the machine.

There seemed to be no message for him conveyed by the nervous tones of

Miss Frayle. Only a lot of rigmarole about the events at the party which took place at the house in Blomfield Road last night. Obviously the young woman was possessed with some delusion that she had the attributes of an amateur detective. He was about to snap off the dictaphone, when he paused a moment longer, fascinated despite himself by the disembodied girlish voice which reached him. Dragging at his cigarette, he leaned against his desk and let the fragrant cigarette-smoke drift round him, while he listened.

He found himself forced to admit grudgingly that she told her story quite well. Nothing extraneous, and the characters, Keaping, Blackwood, the girl Collins, came to life as she described them; Blackwood he had seen fleetingly last night. From Miss Frayle's account he was a very contemporary figure, the disillusioned individual doing a job he no longer believed in.

Keaping appeared to be a more complex character; a man who used liquor to blunt the edge of some evil memory, or to blur some present pain. Not lacking in charm, apparently judging by the tone in Miss Frayle's voice when she spoke of him. Carla Collins? Nothing complicated about her, and Dr. Morelle permitted himself a grim smile. What was the present-day phrase the world of television and motion-pictures had coined for women of her sort? Sex-symbol.

He shook his head despairingly, she had come to a worse end than most.

There was a pause on the machine, as if Miss Frayle was marshalling her facts before continuing. Then the sibilant hiss gave place again to her voice. There was the incident in which the Collins girl had appealed to the man, Keaping. '*She turned to Guy Keaping, who'd been looking on at all this, and said for him to tell Dassinget he'd better see her, maybe he could understand then. Later when I asked Keaping what she had meant, he said I must have misunderstood what she was saying, and then he changed the subject.*'

Dr. Morelle stood very still, listening to the voice from the dictaphone. He

143

detected the edge of anxiety in her tone when Miss Frayle referred to Betty Lewis dancing with the Frenchman and asking him the time. Then the business of the lipstick on Dassinget's face.

Involuntarily Dr. Morelle wondered if his old friend, Inspector Hood, had obtained all this information last night. Every inflection in the girlish voice, firm and controlled now, indicated suspicion aimed at this man, Raoul Dassinget. No doubt, Dr. Morelle reflected, his face darkening, she had got it all wrong.

But that didn't alter the fact that she thought she had stumbled upon something of significance. Connected with Dassinget? That was what she made of it. And so, where, he wondered, was she now?

He glanced at the ormolu clock on the mantelpiece. It was nearly one-thirty. The dictaphone was silent now, except for that sibilant hiss once more, and he switched it off. Oddly disturbed, he looked out of the window. A Daimler slid smoothly along Harley Street. The middle-aged man at the wheel might have been a barrister, chairman of a group of successful companies; his face was bland, his eyes shrewd. Dr. Morelle watched the car pass unseeingly. It wasn't like Miss Frayle to be as late as this for lunch.

He turned away from the window, went across to the telephone and got through to Radio House. A minute or two's inquiries gave him the information that Miss Frayle was not there, though she had called in at Guy Keaping's office. No, Raoul Dassinget hadn't been in his office all morning. He wasn't expected in to-day. Miss Frayle had, it appeared, telephoned after leaving Radio House and obtained Mr. Dassinget's address.

No. Dr. Morelle said, he didn't think they need try and find Mr. Keaping but he would like Mr. Dassinget's address. They duly obliged, and Dr. Morelle hung up. He stood for a moment deep in thought. He had not lunched. There was a lot of work to be done. He snarled between his teeth and went out of the study.

Dr. Morelle knew every inch of Central

London, its busy streets, its mean alleys, its mews, its dead-ends. Almost without conscious thought he could find the shortest route between two places. Now he headed the Duesenberg west, crossed Marylebone High Street and drove the entire length of George Street until he came to Seymour Place. He went up Seymour Place, crossed into Lisson Grove and carried straight along Lisson Grove until it crossed St. John's Wood Road. Beyond the traffic lights Grove End Road began.

The tall modern block of flats he sought came into view, and a few minutes later Dr. Morelle was parked in the wide drive-way and his long raking stride took him through the swing doors. A blue-overalled engineer was packing his toolbag. He was whistling, in the close, carpeted atmosphere of the hall the tune sounded limp and mournful.

As Dr. Morelle came across the hall, he plucked the 'Out of Action' notice from the lift doors and opened them ready for Dr. Morelle. 'Self operated,' he said. 'Press the button for the floor you want.'

Dr. Morelle pressed the appropriate button, and the lift after an initial shudder rose slowly upwards. At the third floor Dr. Morelle stepped from it, and set off down the carpeted corridor. He pressed the bell outside the flat and he heard it ringing inside. He waited. No one came. He rang again, impatiently, but there was no reply.

The thought that he had come upon a fruitless errand afforded him a good deal of irritation. Suddenly he heard the most curious noise. He listened again. It was distant, and muffled, but it sounded like someone shouting and banging. He went along the corridor, trying to locate the noise. It was getting louder. He saw the sign: 'Emergency Stairs.' Now the banging was frenzied, urgent.

Half way along the dark corridor was a tall cupboard. Its door was shuddering with the bangs that came from inside. From the corner of his eye Dr. Morelle glimpsed the emergency staircase, bare and twisting down into the shadows. There was a sudden movement in the gloom and a white shape streaked towards him, turned aside and disappeared in the direction whence he had come. One of the tenants' cats he presumed and returned his attention to the cupboard door.

The key was in the outside of the door. Dr. Morelle turned it, pulled the door open and Miss Frayle fell forward into his arms.

12

Dr. Morelle supported Miss Frayle's dusty, trembling figure, while she gasped: 'How wonderful of you to come. I thought I'd never get out.'

He surveyed her dishevelled state. 'Never mind that,' he said. 'How did you get in?'

The cupboard was full of brooms, buckets, dustpans, scrubbing-brushes. Miss Frayle's head was aching so that she felt it must split open, she knew her face was streaked with tears and dirt, but she didn't care. It was wonderful to be standing there in the corridor, with Dr. Morelle. 'You've saved my life,' she said.

'Someone else could hardly have failed to hear the noise you were making,' he said drily. 'It was not inconsiderable.'

'He must have pushed me in there after he knocked me out.'

'After he what?' He frowned at her. 'We'll get back to the car, and you can tell me what all this is about.'

They travelled down in the lift, while Miss Frayle babbled her story, although her aching head made it difficult to think very clearly. She could not fail to realize, however, with ever increasing chagrin what a fool she'd made of herself.

Dr. Morelle said nothing, he merely regarded her with one dark eyebrow slightly raised. She felt sure he was full of amused contempt for her, and she was forced to admit to herself she could hardly expect him to feel otherwise.

She was quite unaware that as his glance took in her dishevelled figure, he was, in fact, not unaware of a feeling of some compassion. His sardonic expression masked a genuine sympathy as they went across the foyer, out through the swing doors, and he opened the door of the Duesenberg for her. She gulped the fresh air gratefully, gave a tremulous sigh, and groped in her pocket for a handkerchief. It was inadequate, but she wiped her face with it and exclaimed with dismay when she saw the amount of dust that had come off on it.

'But how did you know I was here?' she said to Dr. Morelle miserably. 'Did you come to see him?'

He leaned back without answering her and lit a Le Sphinx. Miss Frayle went over it all again in her mind, as the Duesenberg drew away and headed back to Harley Street. Dr. Morelle had obviously decided that there was nothing to be gained by making any inquiries at Grove Mansions, no doubt he had too little to go on.

She was remembering again the squeaking footsteps that had followed her up the stairs, she heard once more the voice that had called her name when she was outside the flat. A man's voice, which she had felt convinced belonged to Raoul Dassinget. Surely that slight accent had been unmistakable? Then she had gone towards the emergency staircase, suddenly seen the figure in the shadows.

Yet there was something she had forgotten, she felt sure. Some incident which the blow on her head seemed to have wiped from her memory, at least temporarily. She gave up trying to recall what it was as she shivered in the sunshine.

'I don't know how long I was in there, but it felt like hours,' she said to Dr. Morelle, as he swung the Duesenberg round the roundabout opposite Lord's. 'What I can't understand,' she said earnestly, 'is who would have done such a thing to me.'

'The voice sounded like his?' Dr. Morelle said. 'Yet why should Dassinget have been so anxious to prevent your visit?'

'Something in his flat he didn't want me to see?'

'Or someone.'

'Who could that be?'

Dr. Morelle shrugged. 'A number of conjectures offer themselves.'

He seemed unconvinced, but Miss Frayle had latched on to his suggestion, the notion of some mysterious figure waiting in Dassinget's flat made an irresistible appeal to her imagination. 'He knew this someone was already in there, waiting for him,' she said thoughtfully. 'Perhaps he'd seen me on my way in, and he came up the emergency stairs to make sure that the door shouldn't be opened to me by whoever was inside?' She turned to Dr. Morelle, but he seemed to be absorbed in negotiating the turn out of the park into Marylebone Road. 'So he decoyed me away,' she said, 'then knocked me out.'

She thought about it for a moment and then began racking her brains over the identity of whoever had been waiting in the flat at Grove Mansions for Dassinget's return. Who could it be that he was so terrified of her meeting? Once more she tried to recall that memory that eluded her so frustratingly. But all she got was the painful ache in her head, and she gave it up.

Arrived at Harley Street, Miss Frayle's headache was if anything rather worse; Dr. Morelle examined the side of her head, satisfied himself that there was nothing more serious than a bruise caused by the blow she had received, probably from a violent punch with a fist, or perhaps a heavy walking-stick. He packed her off upstairs with a glass of warm milk and aspirin, and a stern order to her not to stir from her bed for the rest of the day.

Some hour or so later when Dr. Morelle had snatched a quick lunch, the burly figure of Detective Inspector Hood stood in the doorway of the study at Harley Street, the inevitable blackened briar-pipe jutting out from beneath the iron-grey moustache.

Dr. Morelle offered him a Le Sphinx. This was not altogether a matter of polite hospitality on his part, Inspector Hood smoked a brand of shag which was inclined to make Dr. Morelle's delicate nostrils twitch. As usual the other rejected the invitation, clutching his pipe.

'I'll stick to this,' he said. 'No point in changing poisons in mid-stream.' He glanced at the door as Dr. Morelle closed it. 'By the way, where's Miss Frayle? She told you, of course, about last night?'

Dr. Morelle nodded as he lit his own cigarette. 'I am sure she will regret having missed you,' he said. 'But she's confined to her bed.'

'I'm sorry to hear that. Bit of a chill?

Or is it the result of last night's excitement?'

'Someone hit her over the head. Probably a punch with a fist.'

Inspector Hood stared at him with mingled sympathy and incredulity. 'Poor Miss Frayle. When did this happen?'

'Early this afternoon. The same person who attacked her then pushed her into a cupboard and locked the door. Had I not chanced to find her, she might be there still.'

And Dr. Morelle explained what had transpired, while the man from Scotland Yard listened his teeth clamped over his pipe-stem, his face grim. Dr. Morelle ended his account and Inspector Hood puffed out a cloud of tobacco-smoke and shook his head uncomprehendingly. 'But why should he want to attack her? And why did she go there to try and see him?'

Dr. Morelle shrugged. 'You know Miss Frayle. A somewhat unpredictable creature at any time. It would appear that my absence abroad, brief as it was, and her spell of employment with these people at Radio House has filled her head with ideas of striking out for herself, particularly in matters which hardly concern her.'

'As a result,' Inspector Hood said and could not resist a broad grin, 'this chap struck out for himself.'

'From what I can deduce,' Dr. Morelle said slowly, 'she was prompted in her action by having decided that this man Dassinget had no alibi for the time of the girl's death.'

The detective rasped his square chin with his pipe-stem. 'He told me he was dancing with someone at the party, a young woman named Lewis, from about 10.45 until 11 o'clock.'

Dr. Morelle moved to the dictaphone. 'Even though Miss Frayle is unable to be here in person,' he said, 'at least you may enjoy the pleasure of listening to her disembodied voice.'

He switched on and Inspector Hood sat down while Miss Frayle's light tones once more filled the study. He gave an occasional grunt of interest as the voice continued against the sibilant hiss of the spinning cylinder. When it ended, his pipe was cold, and he struck a match and held it to the charred bowl. 'Not bad,' he said. 'Not at all bad. Quite following in your footsteps, isn't she?'

'I'm sure Miss Frayle will be delighted to learn of your approval,' Dr. Morelle said.

'Only thing is,' Inspector Hood said, 'it doesn't tell me more than I already know.'

'Miss Frayle has since informed me that this morning, before her ill-advised visit to this man's flat, she went to Radio House, where she learned that, in fact, the young woman, Lewis, must have left Blackwood's house several minutes after eleven p.m.'

'That's not what she told me,' Inspector Hood said, frowning. 'She said she'd left to catch her train a few minutes before eleven.'

'The train which she missed,' Dr. Morelle said, through a cloud of cigarette-smoke.

The other glanced at him sharply. Then he said: 'But why should she deliberately lie to me?'

'She may not have done so deliberately.

She may have believed she was telling you the truth.'

'I don't quite catch on.'

'Dassinget may have informed her incorrectly about the time when she asked him. Remember?'

The man from Scotland Yard stared at him for a moment, chewing at the well-chewed stem of his pipe, which had grown cold once more. He was hearing once again the salient facts which Miss Frayle had recorded.

She had been upstairs with Keaping, when she'd heard the radio from the adjoining upstairs room, Blackwood's bedroom possibly. She had heard the eleven p.m. time-signal, then a few minutes later she and Keaping had come downstairs and Miss Frayle had seen the Lewis girl dancing with Dassinget. She had asked him the time and they had hurried away.

All this, Betty Lewis had corroborated in a chat she'd had with him this morning. She'd missed her train, she'd said. And Inspector Hood hadn't realized the significance of that. Until now.

'Another word with Dassinget might be useful,' he said. 'His alibi for the time of the girl's death was backed up by what this Betty Lewis told me. And he gave her the wrong time. Why?'

'Perhaps his watch isn't very reliable,' Dr. Morelle said humourlessly.

'Incidentally,' the other said, 'the girl had received a severe blow on the back of the skull, the drowning occurred afterwards.'

Dr. Morelle nodded, and Inspector Hood continued as if thinking aloud. 'The only other person without an alibi for 10.45 p.m.' he said, 'is Blackwood himself. He says he went upstairs to his own room, to hear the late news, and Miss Frayle hearing the radio confirms this. And Miss Frayle was hit on the head, too.'

Dr. Morell leaned contemplatively against the writing-desk, cigarette-smoke curling up through his fingers. Inspector Hood said to him: 'You say she identified Dassinget from his voice as the man who decoyed her?'

'She was fairly confident of it. But a

French accent is not hard to assume.'

'So either it was him, and he didn't want her to go to his flat at that particular moment, which suggests he had a visitor. Or else it was someone else, someone who did not want her to see Dassinget.' He glanced narrowly at the tall, cadaverous figure facing him. 'Anyway, thanks for the tip-off,' he said, 'and my best thanks to Miss Frayle. I hope she'll be okay soon.'

Dr. Morelle accompanied Inspector Hood to the front door and stood watching the heavy bulk pad away into the thickening mist that had suddenly descended on Harley Street, swirling in from Regent's Park, then he returned to the study.

He stood lost in thought for a few moments, then he went upstairs and non-committally informed Miss Frayle, who was already beginning to feel better, that he would be out for a little while. Leaving her to ponder as best she might on the reasons for his absence, he quitted the house, and headed the Duesenberg through the misty veils that wrapped

London, in the direction of Radio House.

Into Oxford Street and through Soho, where the fog was patchy, past the huddled offices and wholesale firms of Long Acre the Duesenberg nosed its way. Then down past the busy market-halls of Covent Garden, where the gutters were strewn with discarded fruit and debris.

Dr. Morelle drew up outside Radio House and a few minutes later he was in an office on the sixth floor. It was an office like any other office, with that impersonal, characterless quality, which no amount of photographs pinned to the walls or well-known radio personalities, could give any feeling.

He turned as a voice said: 'Hello, Dr. Morelle. Sorry I had to dash out for a moment. I'm Doug Blackwood. Miss Frayle with you?'

Dr. Morelle eyed the other who was smiling at him, a lazy, cynical smile which quite typified his approach to life. 'Miss Frayle is, to the best of my knowledge, safely in bed, recovering from an accident.'

'Accident? What happened?'

'Someone hit her on the head and knocked her unconscious,' Dr. Morelle said.

'I am sorry,' Doug Blackwood glanced at his watch. 'Look here, I'm due in the studio. Would you care to come and watch? Then you could tell me what happened.'

Dr. Morelle followed Blackwood along the corridor that led to the studio. 'Not a specially fascinating programme. A routine job. It's aim,' he said cynically, 'is the portrayal to our overseas audience of the British way of life.'

He was pushing open a heavy door, and Dr. Morelle found himself in a thickly carpeted foyer. Disposed about it were arm-chairs and small tables, leading off the foyer were six doors, each with a small porthole window at eye level. They were numbered, and above each were two coloured light bulbs, blue for rehearsal, red for transmission.

'Studio 3 for us,' Doug Blackwood said, and led the way into a large control-room with the standard broadcasting equipment. Control-desk, formidable with its range of potentiometers and dials, bank of gramophone turntables along the wall, with racks over them for records, loudspeaker, special desk for playing slow-speed records, built-in tape recorder.

Dr. Morelle glimpsed several men and women who were in the studio, beyond the glass window. They looked up and waved to Blackwood, who moved across to the control-desk, faded up one of the microphones.

'Hello, studio?' he said. 'Anything exciting to-day?'

One of the men said: 'Slight change of order, I'll come up and tell you.' He had a marked French accent.

'Thanks, Raoul.'

Dr. Morelle looked up sharply, but Doug Blackwood appeared to be absorbed in smiling at someone in the studio. And then the control-room door was pushed open and the man came in, a sheaf of papers in his hand. He began talking to Blackwood, apparently not noticing Dr. Morelle.

Physically unimpressive, thin, angular, a man who must live rather on nerves than physique, Dr. Morelle decided, studying him. A face keenly alive, mobile features; hollow-cheeked, crow's feet round his eyes; a lot of very dark hair springing back in an attractive way from his forehead. Yes, very much a man the women would find appealing.

Blackwood was saying to the Frenchman: 'Go back and give me a bit of level, will you?'

The other went back to the studio. Blackwood tested all his microphones in turn, listening to each speaker, balancing one against the other, telling them where to sit. He was immensely efficient, utterly disinterested in what he was doing. He pressed down the talk-back key and told someone that the French half-hour was coming from there, would be starting in four minutes thirty seconds.

A red light flickered intermittently in acknowledgment. In the studio the figures grouped themselves and looked tense. Blackwood leaned casually back in his chair, his eyes on the big clock whose second-hand was jerking round towards transmission time.

Thirty seconds to go. The red light flashed again. Then gave a steady red. Blackwood gave a cue-light to the announcer, faded up the studio microphone, and turned to Dr. Morelle.

'Cigarette,' he said, pulling a crumpled packet from his pocket.

'I would rather smoke my own,' and Dr. Morelle lit a Le Sphinx.

'Now, about Miss Frayle?'

Dr. Morelle recounted briefly the attack upon Miss Frayle at Grove Mansions. Doug Blackwood listened, his eyes straying to the figures in the studio. The needle registering the decibels flickered a little, but stayed constant, as Blackwood held the voices at a uniform level. Dr. Morelle's voice ceased, and Doug Blackwood turned to him, that cynically casual smile on his face.

'Bad luck for poor Miss Frayle,' he said. 'I am sorry.' He glanced through the window again, then back to Dr. Morelle. 'Anyway, you'll be able to have a word with Dassinget, when this is over. The chap who was in here, just before we went on the air.'

13

As Betty Lewis came into the canteen she thought for the thousandth time that it could have been night or day; winter or spring. It was air-conditioned, fluorescent-lighted, not too warm, not too cold. The chairs and tables were gleamingly contemporary. The food-counter was hygienic, the walls were painted in pastel-coloured emulsion paint that could be wiped down. The whole thing was efficient, done to a high standard. The food was average, prices were low.

Betty Lewis sighed and looked glumly round her as she collected a polythene tray and moved along the counter. The white-smocked girl serving her passed her some tea. Betty Lewis eyed the highly-coloured cakes doubtfully, and settled for the most inoffensive-looking one in view. She paid at the desk and moved out into the big room looking for someone to have her tea with.

She was short-sighted, a fact of which she was bitterly resentful, and the far side of the canteen dissolved into a bright blur. It was a continual needless agony to her, this struggle to see. She had spectacles, but she refused to wear them. No one here, in fact, even knew of her disability. It was her private cross, and one she found hard to bear. Contact lenses were too expensive, and anyway, the idea somehow repelled her.

Raoul Dassinget knew she was as blind as a bat. He had come across her one afternoon, when she had been sitting in Victoria Embankment Gardens, reading in the after-lunch sunshine. It was quite a chance encounter and he was sitting next to her before she had time to whip her glasses into her handbag. He hadn't smiled at her dismay and embarrassment. He hadn't made any comment or referred to the glasses at all. He had been friendly, attentive. He had asked her to go dancing with him.

From that moment, the instinctive dislike she had taken to him from the moment of their first meeting had given place to a girlish, wondering admiration. That, in its turn, was quickly to be replaced by a heady infatuation that entirely disregarded his reputation which had gathered about him from promiscuous love-affairs.

Inside a week she slept with him. He was her first man, and he had a searing impact on her. Twenty-seven years old, jealous already of the younger set, rather plain, she went headlong into the attachment. His sexual brutality, his fierce demands upon her emotions, numbed her at first, before she found herself suddenly warmed into a response she had not believed possible.

Everything changed for her. She did her work at Radio House in a daydream, she was aware of no one except him. Life was meeting him, going to his flat. Between these times, it had no meaning at all. At the mere sound of his name, her skin tingled, her blood raced. When she saw him, she trembled so that sometimes she could hardly control her limbs.

With some idea of hugging her pleasure to herself, she had continued to deride him to those about her, she had gained a curious thrill out of expressing disgust at the way he carried on his amorous exploits. Real or figments of gossip, they were constantly being discussed by those he and she worked with. But soon she found herself unable to maintain the pretence, she doted on him in public as well as in private. He seemed to take it all for granted.

Dimly, Betty Lewis now saw Doug Blackwood's solid figure approaching her direction as she found herself a table. She liked him. Before Raoul, she had entertained a certain yearning sometimes for Blackwood.

'You met his nibs?' he said to her, pausing at her table with a cup of tea.

'Who?' she said, and indicated for him to join her.

'The one and only Dr. Morelle, of course,' he said, sprawling into a chair beside her. She glanced at him sharply and saw his casual smile. A sudden fear took possession of her, she wanted to get to her feet and start running. Her hand was perfectly steady as she sipped her tea.

'What, for Pete's sake, does he want, nosing around here?'

'You've answered your own question,' he said, stirring his tea with apparent absorption, and without looking at her. 'He's nosing around.'

She thought he was starting to say something more, then a figure hovered hazily before her. It was Bill Scott, who without asking, pulled out a chair from her table and flopped into it. He looked more gaunt than ever, his eyes were dark-ringed with misery. He took quick, nervous gulps of tea and crammed some chocolate-biscuit into his mouth. His jaws worked stiffly as if they had been out of use for some time. He mumbled something to the two others, and kept glancing at the door then he looked anxiously at the canteen clock.

'What's the hurry?' Betty Lewis said to him sourly. 'You've finished for to-day, haven't you?'

Bill Scott glanced at her, as if surprised that his manner appeared noticeable. He pushed the remainder of the chocolate biscuit into his mouth while he mumbled again. This time it sounded as if he was in a hurry to see someone.

'Who's worth giving yourself dyspepsia for?' Doug Blackwood said evenly.

'Who d'you think?' Scott said bitterly. 'I can't go on any longer. I've got to have a showdown.'

'Oh?' Blackwood said, infusing only slight interest into his tone. Betty Lewis's face seemed to have become pinched and tense. She blinked and toyed with the piece of cake on her plate.

'Are you getting at Raoul?'

It was as if the other had jerked into life, but instead of turning upon Betty Lewis, he spat out the words at Blackwood: 'I know you couldn't care less, even though she died under your own roof.'

Doug Blackwood looked at him mildly, as if to ask what he had done to deserve this gratuitous attack. 'Really,' he said calmly, 'why shoot off your mouth at me? I'm as upset by it as you are. But gunning for Raoul isn't going to help.'

'I'd like to kill him,' Bill Scott's voice was low now, intense. 'I'd like to knock the living daylights out of him.'

'Mind of I sit down?'

The three of them looked up. Guy Keaping was standing behind Scott's chair, looking at them curiously. He had appeared out of the blue. None of them said anything, and the heavy-featured man put down his cup of tea and sat in a chair next to Betty Lewis. Bill Scott was on the other side and he faced Blackwood.

Keaping was eyeing Scott's hands, they were shaking. Not a brave character, he thought. He had caught the other's tight-lipped outburst and he thought privately that he was scared stiff at the prospect of tackling Raoul Dasinget, even with words. Scott jerked up his head and pushed his chair back. Betty Lewis looked at him. So did Doug Blackwood. So did Guy Keaping.

The desperate-faced young man standing there stared across at the canteen clock. Then he walked off, he appeared to be stumbling a little, as he went out of the door. Betty Lewis made as if to go after him, but she was halted by Blackwood.

'Not to worry,' he said, 'Raoul can take care of himself.'

'I wasn't thinking of that,' she said. 'I'm afraid Raoul might — '

'Shove his words down his throat? He has it coming, leave it alone.'

Guy Keaping said nothing, but finished his tea quickly, then he lit a cigarette. Betty Lewis remembered that Bill Scott's arrival had interrupted Doug Blackwood's comments about Dr. Morelle being at Radio House. 'Did Dr. Morelle speak to you?' she said to him.

Blackwood glanced at her. 'He came into the control-room,' he said. 'I was going to introduce him to your boyfriend — '

'Raoul — ?'

The other nodded. 'But he said he wouldn't wait. I thought that was what he'd popped in about — '

'Why should he — ?'

The girl's plain face was pinched-looking again. Her eyes were starting from her head. Blackwood shrugged inconsequentially. 'Dunno,' he said. 'Just a sort of idea he gave me.' He looked at the other man, whose hands were pushed into his pockets, cigarette drooped loosely from the corner of his mouth. 'He see you?'

Keaping stared at him slowly, almost mockingly, then he took the cigarette out of his mouth. 'Dr. Morelle? What's he got on me, that he'd want to gab over?'

Doug Blackwood's expression darkened, there was a definite jeering edge to Keaping's voice, and he didn't like it all that much. 'How should I know?' he said lightly. 'We've all of us got some skeleton hidden away in the back of the old cupboard.'

Again that steady unblinking look. 'You speak for yourself,' Guy Keaping said. He stubbed out his cigarette and Betty Lweis noticed that it was only half-smoked. 'As for Dr. Morelle,' he said, 'what the devil's this business got to do with him? This is Scotland Yard's cup of tea, not his. But, anyway, why should you assume he's prying around? No one's said it's actually murder, not yet.' He paused and in a more dubious tone said: 'Although, I must admit — '

'I have news for you,' Doug Blackwood said, pulling a newspaper which had been folded up in his jacket pocket. He handed it to the other man, pointing to the stop press. Betty Lewis gave a little gasp and read the item. Keaping's expression didn't change as he narrowed his gaze over the early evening edition. It was a cryptic news-story to the effect that Scotland Yard were now convinced that the death of Carla Collins at the house in Blomfield Road was no accident. It was murder.

'In that case,' Guy Keaping said without looking at either of the others, 'I think I'll be getting along.'

They watched him saunter out of the canteen. The girl turned to Blackwood a question on her tongue. 'I thought you knew,' he said, anticipating what she was going to ask him.

'It was pretty obvious to me, as it must have been to everyone,' she said. 'But I suppose I sort of hoped.' She shrugged. 'Not that I'd waste any tears over that little piece.' She glanced down again, and then said: 'Why don't you like him?'

'Keaping? What makes you think that?'

'Come off it,' she said. 'You damn well know you don't. You're hard, aren't you? No use for anyone who's gentle.'

'I wouldn't have called Guy Keaping gentle,' the other said drily. 'Weak if you like.'

'I'm beginning to think the two words mean the same thing.' She sighed heavily. 'Everybody's so ruthless these days. It's every man for himself.'

'And every girl too,' he said. 'Always has been, always will be.' They walked out of the canteen together into the corridor that led to the studios. The girl went through the door of Studio 3D. The man pushed his way into 3E.

Betty Lewis had received the script of the programme she was working on some hours ago. The programme engineer left the preliminaries to her, he would handle the microphones, but the spot-effects would be her particular job. She went through into the studio, where some of the more punctual members of the cast had already arrived. 'Who's narrating?'

she said to an actor. 'It's been left blank on my script.'

The man thumbed through his script. 'Raoul Dassinget,' he said.

Her heart leapt. She could not keep the joy out of her face. She had not known he was to take part in the programme. Then she glanced round. He hadn't arrived yet. She saw the actor smiling at her and guessed that he was one of the many who knew about her and Dassinget, he was grinning at her knowingly. She turned and went back into the control room.

She was in a happy trembling daze, watching the studio through the big window. The prospect that he would walk in, and would glance up and see her, and she would see his dark, ravaged face made her feel sick and faint with longing. She felt a movement behind her, and she twisted round. It was the programme-engineer, a neatly-dressed, balding and fresh-complexioned man. She contrived to smile a welcome to him.

He didn't smile back. His pink face was serious, he was a little out of breath, as if he'd been running, or was excited about something. They had worked together often, they quite liked each other, mainly because they appreciated that each knew the job they did backwards. He, too, knew about her and Dassinget.

She was so thrilled with the news that Raoul was on the programme, that she started to say something to him about it. 'Raoul is on — '

He cut across her excitement-filled words. 'Betty, can you stand a shock? He's dead. He was found a few minutes ago.'

14

She stood there, staring at him as if she had been petrified. For a moment, she thought it was some kind of horrible joke.

'Fell from his office-window,' the man was saying.

And then she screamed, an ugly, long-drawn-out screech of pain. He took her by the shoulders and shook her roughly. 'Stop it, for heaven's sake, stop it.'

The noise ended as abruptly as it had begun. She stared dry-eyed at him. Something seemed to click in her brain. 'Blackwood,' she said in a moan. 'Doug Blackwood.' She stood swaying in the middle of the control-room, her face the colour of putty, vaguely aware of the faces beyond the sheet of glass fixed on her, as the engineer hurried out. She didn't know why she'd asked for Doug Blackwood, some instinct prompted perhaps by the fact that she had only a few minutes before left him, and because he knew Raoul.

The balding man found Blackwood in Studio 3E, and spoke to him hurriedly. 'He's what?' Doug Blackwood gaped at him.

'Dead. I missed seeing it happen by five minutes. I went across the courtyard. Wanted some cigarettes. Saw a huddle of police, people, something under a blanket. Then the police started asking questions. Had anyone seen him fall? Asked me, too. It seems he fell from his office-window.'

Blackwood's face was full of mixed emotions. Then he jerked into action. 'Betty?' he said.

'Next door.'

Blackwood had already pushed the studio door open and went swiftly to the other studio, the pink-faced programme-engineer chasing after him. Betty Lewis was sprawling in a chair at the control-desk, her head down, hidden in her arms. She wasn't crying, just making odd wailing noises. Doug Blackwood went over and gripped her shoulders with his powerful hands.

At once she struggled up, turned a face wildly to him, and then collapsed into his arms. Now she began to sob, while he held her closely and let her cry. 'Where is he?' she said choking. Over her head Blackwood spoke to the other man.

The girl heard the answer and tore herself free from Blackwood and she started for the door.

'Let her go,' Blackwood said, 'I'll look after her.' He followed her out of the studio. She went blindly along the corridor and began to run down the marble staircase. She stumbled, half-way down the stairs. He caught her, gripped her arm. 'Take it easy, Betty,' he said.

She gasped, blinked, coming out of the artificial light of the studios into the bright sunshine of the September afternoon. The courtyard was a square area that lay between the four towering wings of Radio House. It connected by two shallow flights of stone steps with the street. At either entrance a crowd milled around; at one side of the courtyard, directly underneath the window of Raoul

Dassinget's office, a blanket had been spread out. A man rose from his examination, replaced the blanket across the inert shape, and talked to a plain-clothes policeman.

Betty Lewis said something in a quivering voice and ran across the courtyard, Blackwood following her. A uniformed policeman saw her coming and made to stop her. 'Let her through,' Blackwood said. 'She was a friend of his.' The policeman shrugged and let the girl past him. The plain-clothes man turned as she approached, and shot the girl and Blackwood a look from under his eyebrows. 'Not a pretty sight,' he said. 'Fell from that window,' and he nodded upwards.

'Can I see him?' Betty Lewis said. 'Please.'

The man who had been bent over the blanketed shape, and who was a police-surgeon, lifted a corner of the blanket. The girl went over, looked in silence, and then turned away.

'When did this happen?' Doug Blackwood said to the plain-clothes sergeant.

'Twenty minutes past four. His wrist-watch was broken in the fall. No one appears to have seen it happen.'

'I suppose he'd have fractured his skull, falling from that height,' Blackwood said thoughtfully, gazing up at the open window. Faces were leaning out of other windows of the block. Everyone in the place seemed to be staring down at the grim tableau, feasting their eyes on tragedy. Blackwood went across to Betty Lewis and put his arm round her shoulders. 'Let's get out of this,' he said roughly.

She started to say something, but he turned and spoke to the plain-clothes man. 'He was going to get her away from this,' he said, and the other nodded understandingly. 'If you want to get hold of me, or her,' Blackwood said, 'we'll be in my office later.' He gave his and the girl's name and then he steered her up the steps, across the wide thoroughfare, then along one of the side-streets off the Strand that honeycombed that part of London.

'Where are we going?' she asked

without interest. He grinned crookedly. 'Just walk around for a while. Take your mind off things.'

They were in the back streets that flanked Covent Garden. The gutters choked with cabbage-stalks, trodden flat; the atmosphere was pungent with the reek of oranges. Tenement blocks towered above them, their windows blank and dingy. Mothy curtains, white net, cheap cotton print, some windows with no curtains at all. A child's face peeping, white against the glass, sharp-eyed, the face of any slum child. A wireless blared, somewhere above them. Here was the sordid looming back of a theatre. Above them the blue September sky, soon to fade to chill dusk.

His arm was round her shoulders. He liked this part of London, he thought. He liked back streets. They were alive, real. Not just a façade like the pretty shop-windows, he liked rough things, ugly things, unadorned things. He glanced at Betty Lewis. Her tears had stopped, every minute he could put between her and the sight of that blanket-covered shape, would make it easier for her. Control would return, hysteria recede. They passed a public house called the Opera. It wasn't opening time yet. It faced the theatre, across the road. The one so big, imposing with pillars and grand entrance and star bills. The other crouching on the pavement, small and unpretentious.

'I used to walk past this place when I was a kid,' he said to her. 'At nights I used to see the actors troop over from the theatre, trying to make it before closing time. My first job was carrying cups of tea in one of the cafés in the market.' He glanced at her, his eyes narrowed reflectively. 'I was a puny kid then, but when I got to be fourteen, I started to grow, put on muscle. At sixteen I was lifting fruit-boxes as if they were made of cardboard.'

'Quite a way from that to what you arc to-day,' she spoke wearily, she wasn't really interested in what he'd been telling her. She didn't want to know about him, or anyone else. Except someone who was now dead.

'Not so far,' he said. 'Only across the

Strand, that's all.'

They walked back down Drury Lane. It was quiet, above the dismal blocks of flats the late September sky was dusky blue. Here and there a light came on at the back of a shop or dotted about the façades of the buildings. Flowers bloomed in the window-box of a flat they passed, stunted London flowers thriving somehow against a setting of grey walls.

'Now, why don't you go off home? I'll get back and explain you're not feeling too good.'

She shook her head. 'I'd rather walk a little more. I couldn't sit at home.' She closed her eyes as if to shut out the memory of the sight of that inert shape under the blanket. He glanced at her and took her arm more firmly. He wondered what was happening back at Radio House. He imagined the cops would be scurrying about the place by now, asking questions. He wondered if it would look a bit awkward for him and the girl beside him, the way they had taken off and not come back.

He looked at the girl again, her face

deathly white and set, her mouth a thin, bitter line of misery and despair. He shrugged to himself. What did it matter? If the police wanted to talk to either of them, they would be able to later. He stopped in his tracks and Betty Lewis suddenly jerked back and looked up at him.

'What?'

She saw his gaze fixed ahead and she followed it. A tall, angular figure which had appeared round a corner, was approaching them. Black and formidable against the quiet, shadowy street, the figure appeared to be bearing down upon them inexorably.

'Hello, Dr. Morelle,' Doug Blackwood said, 'fancy meeting you.'

Dr. Morelle stood in their path and regarded him and Betty Lewis from under the brim of his soft hat slanted rakishly over one eye. His expression was mild and abstracted. A thin spiral of smoke curled upwards from his cigarette.

'You know about — ?' Betty Lewis said, and her voice broke off.

Dr. Morelle inclined his head.

'You on your way to Scotland Yard, hot-foot?' Blackwood said.

Dr. Morelle who had been observing Betty Lewis's pallor and tense features, turned to eye him coolly. 'I shall be calling there in due course. I found the atmosphere of Radio House a trifle close and depressing,' he began, but Blackwood interrupted him.

'You can say that again,' he said. He looked at the girl, as if wondering if he should say what was in his mind. 'About Dassinget, did you see him after the broadcast?'

'What did you want to see him about?' Betty Lewis said, cutting in. 'What had you got to do with him?' Her voice rose fiercely and Doug Blackwood gripped her arm warningly. But she went on. 'Or did he ask you to call?'

'Unfortunately, I wasn't acquainted with him to that extent,' Dr. Morelle said. He glanced at Blackwood. 'I didn't see him. I was about to say that I left you, while the programme was proceeding,' and the other gave a nod, 'with the object of obtaining a little fresh air.

Unfortunately I missed Dassinget.'

Blackwood's face was withdrawn. Was he reflecting, Dr. Morelle wondered, that if he hadn't gone out for that breath of air, but had waited for Raoul Dassinget, the latter might now be alive?

'What did you want to see him about?' Betty Lewis said again, pushing her face forward. 'That's what you haven't told me.'

'I feel bound to ask you,' Dr. Morelle said, 'why you are so concerned about my interest in Dassinget?'

'I loved him,' the girl said, flinging the words at him with tear-choked defiance. 'And he loved me, that's why I'm entitled to know what you were after him about. I suppose it was to do with that damned Collins girl — neither of us have got him, now.'

She burst into an inconsequential tirade, until Blackwood managed to quieten her. Dr. Morelle stood there, silent, his eyes hooded. He was recalling Miss Frayle's reference to Betty Lewis's obvious infatuation with Dassinget. He wondered with a sense of pity, how it was

189

that this plain, neurotic creature could really delude herself that the man whose death must have affected her so shockingly had ever really felt any affection for her.

He said quietly to Blackwood: 'May I suggest that you get her home and see that she is given a sedative?'

Doug Blackwood agreed that it would be the best plan, and the girl watched the tall, dark figure move away with long raking strides.

They could not have known that Dr. Morelle, proceeding in the direction of the Duesenberg where he had parked it, held in his mind's eye the picture of Raoul Dassinget as he had last seen him a short while ago. That crumpled figure, its neck grotesquely twisted.

But along the line of the jaw Dr. Morelle had discerned a bruise, the sort of bruise that could have been caused by a blow, struck with a powerful fist.

15

'Did he fall or was he pushed? That's the question, as William Shakespeare would say.' Inspector Hood clenched his teeth over his pipe-stem and turned back from the window of his office to regard Dr. Morelle who sat quietly by the plain, tidy desk.

It was some half-an-hour later, after Dr. Morelle's encounter with Doug Blackwood and Betty Lewis in the neighbourhood of Covent Garden. From Whitehall and the Embankment the combined rumble of the traffic carrying London's workers homewards, the day's work done, reached the cramped office at Scotland Yard. The bright electric light was hazed by the mist of smoke from Inspector Hood's pipe and Dr. Morelle's cigarette.

Dr. Morelle had found on arrival that Inspector Hood himself had only recently returned from Radio House, where he had hurried on receiving the news of Raoul Dassinget's fatal fall. Dr. Morelle had duly acquainted the bulky detective with all the information he had to offer him.

'You agree, of course, that this links up with last night's spot of bother at Blomfield Road?' Inspector Hood advanced upon Dr. Morelle and jabbed his pipe-stem at him.

'There would appear to be obvious connection between the two occurrences,' Dr. Morelle said. 'That is, assuming that Dassinget was pushed.'

'That's what my money's on.' The Scotland Yard man sat down heavily at his desk and pored over a folder. As he frowned to himself, he went on, talking his ruminations aloud. 'That bruise on his jaw you spotted, our sawbones here confirms it was inflicted before death. He could have fallen backwards, but there's a radiator just under the window and he'd be pretty unlikely to go right over the top of the radiator.' He passed a slip of paper across to Dr. Morelle. 'Found this in his pocket.'

Dr. Morelle held it delicately between finger and thumb. It was a cheque for twenty-five pounds. He regarded the sprawling signature intently. Then he sat back as Inspector Hood said: 'This throws new light on the matter.'

'It may be the answer.' He put the cheque down on the desk and watched Inspector Hood pick it up and then return his attention to the folder before him.

'Dassinget was found at 4.22 p.m.,' he said. 'Death had only just occurred when the body was found. The broken wrist-watch suggests he fell from the window at 4.20 p.m.'

Dr. Morelle agreed that the times fitted in with the time when the programme he had witnessed in the process of being broadcast, in which Dassinget was concerned, must have ended.

'Now,' Inspector Hood said, 'who was in the neighbourhood of his office between 4.15 and 4.20 p.m.?'

'Tell me,' Dr. Morelle said.

'That's the trouble. I can't tell you a lot. Take this chap Bill Scott.' He regarded the folder again. 'Hated Dassinget's guts. Admits it. At four p.m., or thereabouts was in the canteen swearing he was going to kick Dassinget's teeth in. Or words to that effect. The girl, Betty Lewis and Doug Blackwood — you met them — and the other man, Guy Keaping, agreed on this. They were there when he said it.'

'A rather plain, but forceful young woman,' Dr. Morelle said.

'Keaping says he called at Dassinget's office, about 4.15 p.m. Said he wanted to ask his advice about some point in a script. Says he saw Bill Scott near the office when he came out. And Scott is a bit involved in the carryings-on that preceded Carla Collins' murder. Accused Dassinget of having done it.'

'Quite a tangled skein,' Dr. Morelle said, contemplating the tip of his cigarette, while he recalled that Miss Frayle had been struck down at Grove Mansions by a blow from a fist.

'There was a girl in an office nearby, busy rolling off scripts, her office door was shut and she didn't hear anything at all.' Inspector Hood's pipe-stem traced a pattern on a sheet of paper. 'Another typist was working in an office a couple of doors from Dassinget's. Came out of her office about 4.15 p.m. to go down to the canteen. Saw Scott going towards Dassinget's office. Saw another man appear at the end of the corridor. Guy Keaping. Now, Bill Scott admits he went along to give Dassinget a beating-up, but changed his mind. Thought he might be taking on more than he could chew. Went away, he says, without going into Dassinget's office. He confirms he met Guy Keaping when he was going to the office. Time about 4.15 p.m.'

Dr. Morelle remembered that it was this man, Keaping whom Miss Frayle seemed to be rather interested in. A slimly-built youngish man, with a rather dour expression, as if suffering from some secret sorrow. The type, Dr. Morelle was thinking, Miss Frayle would most likely consider not unattractive. A spasm of irritation flickered over his face, so that Inspector Hood, glancing up, said: 'What's biting you, Doctor?'

Dr. Morelle shook his head. 'I was merely considering the possibilities that this list of yours opens up.'

He gave a passing thought to Miss Frayle, wondering if she had recovered from the effects of the blow on her head, as the other said: 'This man, Keaping, says that when he came out again, after only about a couple of minutes with Dassinget, this other chap, Scott, was still there. And that he saw him go into the office.' Dr. Morelle's eyebrow was raised. 'Keaping, who knew Scott had it in for Dassinget, because Scott was in love with Carla Collins.'

'This is what Keaping says?' Dr. Morelle said through a puff of cigarette-smoke.

'This is what Keaping says,' Inspector Hood said. 'Another thing he mentioned was that Blackwood seems to be pretty well off, but nobody knows how he's got the money. He doesn't earn all that at Radio House. And you'll remember that place of his at Blomfield Road?'

Dr. Morelle did remember it, and he smiled to himself at the recollection of the astonishment on Miss Frayle's face when she opened the door and saw him standing there.

'And finally,' Inspector Hood was saying, 'although Doug Blackwood and Betty Lewis corroborate that they each went to their respective studios at about 4.15 p.m., Blackwood nipped out again to buy some cigarettes, he says, a few minutes later. From the canteen.'

'You checked that, naturally?'

'We tried to. But at the time when he says he bought the cigarettes, there was a bit of a panic on in the canteen. One of the girls had dropped a tray full of crockery, and the manageress was tearing off a strip about it to everyone within range. No one remembered exactly who was in and out, just about that time.'

Inspector Hood slowly got to his feet, characteristically rasping his chin with his pipe-stem and moved over to the window. Big Ben chimed and the detective glanced at his watch. 'Six o'clock,' he said. 'I was wondering if you'd care to come along with me to Grove Mansions?'

'If you think I could be of any help,'

Dr. Morelle said, spreading his hands self-deprecatingly. 'I would hate to be in your way.'

The other smiled at him. 'I don't seem to remember any occasion when you were,' he said. 'And, anyway, you might pick up a hint about who it was banged Miss Frayle over the head.' He paused, stuck his pipe between his teeth and struck a match which he applied to the cold bowl. 'I suppose it's occurred to you,' he said, 'that whoever it was did that was pretty free with his fists, and might be the same one who socked Dassinget?'

'It had occurred to me,' Dr. Morelle said.

The detective looked at him. 'I'll be about half-an-hour,' he said. 'Want to go over to the lab and check one or two points. If you'd care to wait, I'll be with you. We might have a drink before we shove off? I could use a scotch.'

And so a few minutes later found Dr. Morelle proceeding out of Scotland Yard, having arranged to meet Inspector Hood at the little public-house nearby, frequented by police-officers and newspapermen, within half-an-hour. On his way out, Dr. Morelle remembered to telephone Harley Street and spoke to Miss Frayle, who informed him that there were no messages for him. Before he rang off he asked her if she was feeling better, and she said she was; but he fancied she sounded a trifle deflated.

He came out into the falling dusk and crossed to the tall gates to turn into New Scotland Yard, heading for Cannon Row. A figure stepped out of the shadows. 'Could you spare me a moment, Dr. Morelle?'

Dr. Morelle spun round. It was Doug Blackwood. He had been waiting for Dr. Morelle, he said. He had seen Betty Lewis on to a train for her home in the suburbs where she lived with her mother, and then he had come along to Scotland Yard, in the hope that Dr. Morelle would be there. He'd been lucky, he said. 'I'm in no haste,' Dr. Morelle said. 'Perhaps you would care to join me for a drink?'

'That's remarkably human of you,' Doug Blackwood said.

'You flatter me,' Dr. Morelle said.

The other grinned. 'I was always a bit under the impression that you were rather on the inhuman side. You know, all mind and not much heart.' The big, tough-looking engineer had fallen into step with Dr. Morelle. 'The idea quite appeals to me, as a matter of fact, I haven't got much time for the human heart myself.'

Dr. Morelle privately wondered what sort of impression of him Miss Frayle must have given her acquaintances at Radio House. No doubt she had created a completely false picture of him as some aloof martinet, forbidding and lacking in any warmth or understanding. His mouth tightened in a thin line. They came out of Cannon Row into Whitehall, which was alive with home-going office workers, some streaming towards the tube station, another current forcing its way to the buses.

'Look at them,' Blackwood said in disgust. 'Swarming ants all scared to death they'll miss the 6.20 p.m. and have to wait for the 6.25. All frightened of getting home five minutes later than usual. Makes you despair for the human race, doesn't it?'

'I cannot say the spectacle has that effect on me,' Dr. Morelle said mildly. 'But then I find it is more rewarding to concentrate on the individual rather than upon the mass. See for instance the woman crossing the road. Certainly she looks worried, even harassed, but there is a quality of intelligence in her face which redeems everything else.'

'How about that bank-clerk, or whatever he is?' Blackwood said. 'Scurrying to buy a paper. Doesn't he sum up the whole futile rush?'

'I see an unhappy man,' Dr. Morelle said, 'a man struggling to keep up appearances in an inflationary world. Observe how shabby are those orthodox office clothes, the neatly darned patch on the elbow of his jacket. The worn-down shoes. Perhaps he has some very good reason for hurrying home. To see his child before she is put to bed. To help an over-worked wife. I do not despise him.'

Doug Blackwood looked at him sharply. 'No point in arguing. Let's admit

I'm intolerant and leave it at that.'

'Intolerance is tempting,' Dr. Morelle said thoughtfully. 'I myself have to struggle against it. But I would suggest that you are confusing intolerance with arrogance. The arrogance of someone who has climbed a certain distance but who rather despises himself for the methods he has adopted to do so.'

Doug Blackwood looked disconcerted, but he contrived to laugh it off. 'What pub are we going to?' he said, as he followed Dr. Morelle out of the crowd and into a narrow quieter street.

The summer-like warmth of the afternoon had abruptly vanished, true autumn chill had sharpened the air. October was only a few days away, the unwelcome return of winter-time. A faint cool breeze blew up from the river. The sky was a melancholy grey-blue. Beside Dr. Morelle, Blackwood made a powerful figure, immensely wide and heavy across the shoulders, long armed, long legged.

When they stepped into the little public-house, they left behind them the bustle of Whitehall. Dr. Morelle had a scotch-and-soda, his companion had a pink gin. The bar was only reasonably busy, and they settled down at a table and eyed each other across their glasses.

'Of course you're right,' Doug Blackwood said presently. 'I've come a long way. And I'm not proud of myself. But I'd like to know how you summed me up.'

Dr. Morelle looked at him, and now his gaze was probing, not easy to meet. Blackwood twirled his glass. 'During a lifetime of the study of the human mind and its workings, I have come to analyse individuals almost without conscious effort.'

'Very useful for you in your job,' Blackwood said.

Dr. Morelle gave a ghost of a smile. 'It also has the unfortunate effect of putting me at a distance from my fellow-men. It is hard to be the intimate of any person whose mind you have dissected.'

'You don't strike me as a man who needs intimates,' the other said. 'You're essentially a lone wolf.'

'Circumstances may have forced that role upon me,' Dr. Morelle said. 'But it is not an enviable one.'

'It must have its compensations. Fame. Money.'

'What are these things?' And Dr. Morelle waved them away with a hand. 'It is the kingdom of a man's mind which dictates whether he is satisfied, and happy.'

'Money doesn't guarantee peace of mind, that's for sure. But it helps you to drown your sorrows all the same.'

'You speak like a man with sorrows to drown,' Dr. Morelle said.

'I've had my share.' The other's face was suddenly hard and his eyes unsmiling. 'Why do you want to know? If it's anything to do with Dassinget, you're unlucky. After Betty Lewis and I saw you earlier, we went back to Radio House. The police were there and I told them all I knew. So did Betty, though it amounted to less than I had to tell them, before I took her to Waterloo for her train.'

'I'm not a police-officer,' Dr. Morelle said quietly.

Doug Blackwood had refused one of Dr. Morelle's cigarettes and had pulled out a packet of his own, and lit up. He inhaled deeply. Suddenly he began talking.

'It was a woman,' he said. 'She was about fifty-five, made-up to look like thirty-five. I met her quite by chance, when I was working in Covent Garden. She was slumming. At first I tried to tell her she was wasting her time. But next day she was there in this café again. And the day after that. She was stinking with money. Damn great house in Chelsea that looked across the river; three cars, all Bentleys. A week later I was installed, nominally I was her chauffeur. She kept me for eighteen months. It came to an end with her death. She left me all her money. There was quite a lot.'

'After your first dismay,' Dr. Morelle said quietly, 'you have found it pleasant to be on your own again?'

Blackwood laughed harshly. 'Are you kidding? I felt like a man who's just got out of prison. I found myself a blonde and beat it to the South of France with her. We went to the casino every night, and every time I lost some of the old girl's money I felt a weight roll off my back.'

'You've got through all of it by this time, no doubt?' Dr. Morelle said drily.

The other shook his head. 'She'd tied it up too securely for that. I've an income for life, whether I like it or not.'

'A somewhat bizarre situation,' Dr. Morelle said. 'A man with money he does not want, yet cannot dispose of.'

'My scruples have worn off. This was a long time ago. I'm happy enough to spend her money now.'

'Why did you wait for me this evening?' Dr. Morelle said. 'Merely to tell me the story of your life, or part of your life?'

Doug Blackwood put down his glass. 'Maybe,' he said slowly. 'Maybe there was some inner compulsion to get it off my chest to someone. But, consciously, I wanted to see you to tell you that Betty Lewis is absolutely in the clear about Dassinget.' Dr. Morelle frowned at him. 'I know it may seem odd, telling you this, but I want you to believe me.'

'What seems odd to me,' Dr. Morelle said, 'is that you fear she should be connected with his death.'

'Somebody was.'

Dr. Morelle's gaze narrowed. 'What makes you think so?'

'Who are you trying to kid?' Blackwood said. 'You know damn well he was murdered.'

'I might ask who gave you that information?'

'She told me. She saw him there, just after he was found. I was with her. She saw him, dead. She saw the bruise on his jaw, Dr. Morelle. Where, whoever it was must have socked him good and hard before they shoved him through the window. But you know about that, you or the police must have spotted that.' He stood up, glancing at his watch. 'I'll be getting along,' he said.

Dr. Morelle got to his feet, glancing at the door, expecting Inspector Hood. 'When did she tell you this?' he asked.

'After we bumped into you, this afternoon. She suddenly blurted it out, she asked me if she should tell you. I told her to keep out of it, that I'd tell you. You see, it proves she didn't do it. Otherwise, she wouldn't have told me. Would she?'

Dr. Morelle nodded thoughtfully. 'In any case,' he said, 'it needed more than a young woman's strength to inflict that blow. It must have been someone much more powerful.'

'I thought you'd catch on,' Doug Blackwood said and turned on his heel and began to move out of the bar.

Dr. Morelle accompanied him into the street. He watched him hail a taxi, saw him get in, saw the cab turn towards Charing Cross. Then, conscious of the need for space about him he walked quickly back towards Scotland Yard, hoping to meet Inspector Hood, and not wishing to wait in the stuffy bar.

The homegoing crowds had dwindled to a trickle. The sky was darkening and the lights everywhere glittered against the gloom, the background of shadowy buildings. He was recalling the ugly story he had been told. Certain points of it came back to his mind. The man's remorse. The old woman's death. Blackwood had collected a lot of money when she died. And he had suffered a bad conscience about it. He had deliberately let it slip through his fingers. Now he felt better about it, now her death was more remote. But was there something else he had wanted to forget? Had there been something else he hated to remember?

Dr. Morelle's reflections tangled with the implications arising out of this second death, following so rapidly upon the murder of Carla Collins, so that it seemed the same hand might be responsible for both. And what was the motive?

As he turned into Cannon Row, he saw a familiarly burly shape approaching, and he quickened his step as he went to meet Inspector Hood.

16

The police-car swung into the lighted drive-in of Grove Mansions. It pulled up outside the main entrance to the flats and Inspector Hood and Dr. Morelle, accompanied by the same plain-clothes sergeant who had been with the detective the previous night, got out and pushed a way through the swing-doors.

The porter looked up from the evening newspaper he was reading. 'I'm Inspector Hood from Scotland Yard, and I'd like to have a look round the late Mr. Dassinget's flat. Can I have the key, please?'

The porter's eyes were sharp with curiosity. 'Dreadful thing, wasn't it?' He tapped a finger against the news item in the paper. 'Him falling out of that window. Only goes to show, you can't never be too careful.' He took a key down from a board on the wall behind him and handed it over. 'Shall I show you the way up?'

'We can find it,' Inspector Hood said, and the man watched them cross to the lift, before he returned with a sigh to his newspaper. Inspector Hood and Dr. Morelle and the sergeant got out of the lift on the third floor and looked about them. 'The place where Miss Frayle was attacked was along there?' Hood said.

Dr. Morelle nodded. 'The passage that leads to the emergency staircase,' he said. 'The voice called her from that direction.'

He led the way to where the emergency staircase spiralled downwards. It was dimly lit. Three floors below, at ground level, they saw it was lighter. Dr. Morelle indicated the cupboard where he had found Miss Frayle, then they followed him along the corridor towards the flat.

Inspector Hood turned the big key in the lock and stepped inside. The flat was in darkness. He switched on the light and looked about him. This was the sitting-room, small and neat, well-furnished. There were standard and table lamps about the room and he went in and began switching them on. The room sprang into life. Two doors led off it. The sergeant, trying them both, found that one went through into a bedroom, and the other led through into a small kitchen. Leading off the bedroom was a small bathroom.

'Must have set him back a fair bit I should say,' Inspector Hood said. 'They don't give places like this away.'

Dr. Morelle was looking around him. He noticed that there was an almost negative atmosphere about the place. It had been, he suspected, merely a *pied-à-terre* for its owner. He had given nothing of himself to it, and now that he no longer occupied it, it had reverted to anonymity. Small bookshelves ran along one wall and the volumes had an untouched appearance.

Dr. Morelle crossed to them to inspect the books but the titles told him nothing. They were the usual hotch-potch a man accumulates over a lifetime. A Shakespeare, an English and French dictionary, two small books on radio technique, written in French, a volume of Marcel Proust, several paper-back novels, with

212

markers inserted at the more colourful descriptions.

Inspector Hood had gone through into the bedroom. A moment later he called to Dr. Morelle. 'Didn't Miss Frayle say that the man who followed her up the stairs had squeaking shoes?'

Dr. Morelle joined the other in the bedroom. The room was as tidy, as impersonal as the sitting-room. A divan-type interior sprung bed; two modern prints hung on the pastel-coloured walls; a wardrobe, clothes-chest, easy chair. Inspector Hood opened the wardrobe door, eyed the row of shoes laid out inside, then called to the sergeant, who came in. 'What size are your feet?'

'Eight-and-a-half.'

'Try these on, they'll be too big but see if any of them squeak.'

Dassinget possessed quite a spectacular fondness for shoes.

There were black ones, brown ones, a flashy pair of tan brogues, and light-soled dancing pumps. Some were down at heel, one pair had broken laces. They were the first sign of humanity in that oddly inhuman flat.

Patiently the plain-clothes man put on one pair of shoes after another and walked up and down. Inspector Hood sat on a corner of the bed and relapsed into gloom. Dr. Morelle watched the pantomime with saturnine humour. None of the shoes squeaked. When it was over, Inspector Hood shook his head.

'Looks like it wasn't him who followed Miss Frayle up the stairs.' He turned to the sergeant, who was putting on his own shoes. 'Remember to check those he was wearing when he died.'

Dr. Morelle accompanied the two men into the sitting-room and watched while they opened the small writing-desk. They took out a handful of documents and were silent, turning over old letters. Dr. Morelle watched Inspector Hood flip through a small notebook. 'This could be something,' he said.

Dr. Morelle glanced over the other's shoulder. 'Regular money payments,' he said musingly. 'And initials written against them. Invariably the same two initials.'

'As though someone was regularly paying him money,' Inspector Hood said.

'And the cheque made out to Dassinget was signed by someone with the same initials,' Dr. Morelle said slowly.

'This may be the lead we want,' Inspector Hood said.

'The cheque was dated the 25th, wasn't it?' Inspector Hood nodded. Dr. Morelle looked at the notebook again. He saw that the amounts entered ranged from twenty to fifty pounds. He saw the last entry. 'It has been entered up,' he said, 'with the initials beside it. Even though Dassinget had not yet paid it in to his bank.'

'If this is blackmail,' Inspector Hood said, 'and from where I'm standing, it smells like it, why didn't whoever it was who killed Dassinget find that cheque? I mean, you'd have expected them to have turned his pockets out, to see if he still had it on him.'

'Doubtless he — or she — imagined that he had paid it in immediately he received it. Which would indicate that he was well acquainted with Dassinget's habits.'

'In that case,' Inspector Hood said, 'why did he kill him? If he wasn't going to get the cheque back?'

'There could be any number of reasons why the murderer chose that particular moment,' Dr. Morelle said.

Inspector Hood, his pipe quite cold and ignored, stood there in a reflective mood, while the sergeant continued his search. 'Who are our suspects?' Inspector Hood said. 'Bill Scott? Had he the guts to go through with it? Guy Keaping, as tough as they come, I'd say. Or the Lewis girl?' He looked grimly at the account book. 'A little chat with the owner of these initials ought to help.'

Dr. Morelle turned his head towards the plain-clothes man, who had just muttered an exclamation. He had been sorting through some letters and snapshots. Now he looked up. 'The name Diana Margaret Morse mean anything?'

Inspector Hood looked across at him, frowning, searching his memory. 'Who is she?'

'Was,' the sergeant said, 'she died couple of years back.' He was looking at several newspaper-cuttings as he spoke. 'Road accident in France, hit-and-run driver.'

Inspector Hood stood beside him and strange gurgling noises came from his pipe as he glanced through the letters and photographs, the newspaper-cuttings which the other showed him.

'He seems to have known her,' he said. He threw a glance at Dr. Morelle, who moved over to him. Inspector Hood passed the photographs across and Dr. Morelle stared at Dassinget's image.

The photographs were amateur efforts, they were mostly of Dassinget. One was of him and the girl arm-in-arm. There were two photographs, very much better in quality, of the girl herself. A dark-haired, pretty girl. On the backs of the photographs of Dassinget was written: Raoul, Trafalgar Square, May 16th. Raoul, at Brighton, June 10th.

Inspector Hood had dug out several letters, they were in girlish handwriting, and Dr. Morelle compared it with the writing on the back of the photographs. The girl in the photos with Dassinget was the same as the girl whose photo was in the newspaper-cuttings. 'He must have acquired them after her death,' he said.

'Why the devil should he keep these and the stuff about an accident in France two years ago?' Inspector Hood said. 'Bit sentimental for his type.'

Dr. Morelle gave him a thin smile. 'Sentiment lingers where you may least expect to find it. What brutal murderer hasn't wept over a dog?'

Inspector Hood gave a grunt of agreement, while Dr. Morelle glanced through the cuttings. They were yellow and tattered, but the story they told was easily pieced together. Inspector Hood muttered aloud over Dr. Morelle's shoulder.

'One of those unsatisfactory jobs they never got to the bottom of. Seems she goes to France with her boy-friend. They quarrel and split up. She starts to hitch-hike back to Paris when she's knocked down and killed. Her boy-friend arrives back in Paris and hears she's been killed.'

The newspaper-cuttings rustled as

Inspector Hood turned them. He read on. 'They never found out who ran her down. Doesn't seem to have been much sympathy for the boy-friend at the inquest. Bit of a cad to ditch his girl two hundred miles from Paris.'

'And his name, of course,' Dr. Morelle said, 'was Dassinget.'

Inspector Hood gave him a look and said thoughtfully. 'That's what doesn't quite add up. I mean, if someone was blackmailing Dassinget, that would fit.'

'On the contrary, Dr. Morelle said. 'The mere fact that his name was publicly coupled with her death, would automatically remove any such threat.'

Inspector Hood considered this, chewing his pipe-stem and scowling to himself. 'Yet,' he said, 'blackmail's mixed up in this. You'll have noticed,' indicating the note-book, 'that these entries started three weeks after this girl was killed.'

'I had noticed that,' Dr. Morelle said.

'His women seem to have been on the unlucky side,' the sergeant said. 'This girl, then Carla Collins.'

Inspector Hood growled something

under his breath. Dr. Morelle was recalling the girl he had encountered with Doug Blackwood earlier that evening. Her white face, her neurotic outburst directed at him. She was another of Dassinget's victims. Though she was alive, her association with him must have brought her little real happiness, only frustration.

Abruptly he picked up his hat, his stick, his gloves. There seemed to be little reason for remaining, and he bade Inspector Hood and the other man good night and quitted the flat, conscious of a growing and violent distaste for the place.

He took a taxi to Scotland Yard, where he had parked the Duesenberg and only when he was driving back to Harley Street did he sigh, and relax. He would be glad to put Dassinget and all that he stood for out of his mind for a few hours. An unpleasant individual, everything he touched had been smeared with tragedy of some kind. Some men were like that, they left a trail of misery and destruction behind them. Usually, like Dassinget, they were attracive on the surface, gay, irresponsible; the extent of the damage they caused might only be measured afterwards. When it was too late.

It was a moonless evening, the sky black and utterly without stars. Dr. Morelle felt a rare claustrophobia in the London streets. He longed for the visual solace of a wide sweep of landscape. His thoughts went back to his Scandinavian trip, and the pale nights of illimitable space. Even against the blackest of nights the outline of hills and woods, of the sea against the Northern horizons stood out clear. His ears, jaded with the throb of car-engines, the hum of the city, ached for the rustle of pines in a night-wind, the chatter of birds gathering for migration in a lonely wood.

Like some dispossessed spirit he drove towards Harley Street. He drove quickly, with none of his usual enjoyment of being at the wheel of his beloved Duesenberg, his mind returning to the work that awaited him. Miss Frayle's injury, he thought grimly, could not have happened at a more inconvenient time.

As he swung the Duesenberg into

Harley Street he experienced a sense of gladness, perhaps it wasn't so bad being home, after all. He hurried into the house, he would have a drink, he decided, or coffee and then work. For him to go to bed before one o'clock in the morning was utterly useless. He slept little, and never before the small hours.

He mixed himself a stiff whisky-and-soda and paced the study, glancing idly at the bookshelves and filing-cabinets that filled the walls. Here were the dossiers and text-books in French, German and Italian, as well as English, all devoted to his work, the study of the human mind under the shadow of violence and lust, the motives and compulsions that entangled the human spirit in the meshes of greed and murder, avarice and villainy.

He lit a Le Sphinx and watched the smoke curl up in the light from the standard lamp. Even now, with his mind ceaselessly humming, he could control his body, force it to rest. He sat down at his desk and sank in a reverie, then he got to his feet and crossed to the door. On the way to the hall he paused, and went into the laboratory.

He stood on the threshold and with the light switched on glanced round. It was a relatively small laboratory which he had devised and had constructed to suit his particular purpose. Every inch of space was fully taken up with the most up-to-date equipment. Gleaming steel and glass caught his eye everywhere, on the shelves and benches and in the glazed cupboards, copper and aluminium and porcelain basins and beakers. Flasks, specimen jars and miscellaneous pipettes.

He gave an approving look at the micro-analysis apparatus which he had designed himself incorporating his own improvements. Retorts and bulbs, crucibles and test-tubes gleamed and winked. Test-tubes and funnels, syphons and condensers. He checked the time by his wrist-watch with the synchronous clock silenty ticking away the seconds, which faced him on the opposite wall.

He thought of the analytical precision scales which he had seen in the police laboratory at Oslo. His eyes narrowed a trifle enviously as he thought how well it would look here. Making a mental note to inquire after it from the firm who usually supplied him with similar instruments, he switched out the light and closed the laboratory door behind him.

He had wondered abstractedly if Miss Frayle might have been occupied with the note he had left on his desk, but it seemed that she had not recovered sufficiently from her ordeal of the afternoon. For once, he thought, with an ironic twitch at the corners of his mouth, she was obeying him. Not a bit like her.

He frowned to himself. Should he go upstairs and see if she was in fact all right? He hesitated. It was late, for her. She might well be asleep. Finally he started up the stairs, and was rapping quietly at her door. There was no sound from within. He called out in a low voice: 'Miss Frayle? Are you all right?'

There was no answer. It occurred to him that she might have recovered sufficiently to go out, following another of her foolish impulses. He felt oddly disturbed. He put out a hand and tried the door, opening it a few inches.

'Miss Frayle? Are you there?'

Still there was no sound. There was a shaft of darkness where the door stood open. He was about to call more loudly, when he decided that he was being unnecessarily anxious. He felt convinced that she was fast asleep, the possibility of her having flagrantly disobeyed him really was out of the question. He was realizing how little he knew about her life outside her job, about her friends, her interests. She had been an efficient secretary and that was enough. How she filled her time had not concerned him. Only now was he beginning to wonder a little about her.

Since her return from working at Radio House, he realized with grim humour, since she had escaped from his influence and come under that of people like this man Blackwood and this other individual Guy Keaping. And, of course, all this abnormal excitement raging round the deaths of the girl and the Frenchman. He started down the stairs again, slowly. Once he stopped, and listened. The house was silent, only the subdued tick of the clock downstairs.

He halted once more. For a fleeting moment he thought he heard the squeak-squeak of a shoe as if someone was ascending the stairs. He waited, listening, but he failed to hear the noise again. His mind went back to Miss Frayle's account of her visit to Grove Mansions, her description of what had transpired before she had been attacked. He recalled how the plain-clothes man had later padded up and down Dassinget's flat in the Frenchman's shoes, without getting a squeak out of them.

Dr. Morelle went into his study, closed the door thoughtfully and crossed to the desk. He switched on the desk-lamp, stared before him, eyes narrowed; then he turned to the mass of notes and within a few moments he had forgotten Miss Frayle, Dassinget and Blackwood, Betty Lewis and Inspecor Hood. And the two murders.

17

By night the place was as different from its daytime self as a hospital ward is different.

The lights were burning, the sense of controlled activity was as strong as in the daytime hours, people hurrying about their business; but the clamour and bustle of the day was muted.

Here as in a hospital, some slept, waiting an early morning call; others, the night-shift, took no heed of the darkness outside the windows, for them, the night had its pattern of broadcasts, just as the day. The words they spoke into microphones here in London, in the small hours of the morning, would be received in the full brilliance of daylight, in remote parts of the world.

Those who sensed the importance of their jobs liked working at night, there were fewer staff on duty; responsibilities were greater, it was easier to imagine in the still hours of the night the remote audience listening in far parts of the world. Those who were disillusioned, cynical, found night-shifts the most futile part of their work.

To sit in the broadcasting studio at two o'clock in the morning, working in something that was dead on its feet seemed the height of idiocy. The only compensation, perhaps, was that they could dream of what might have been, the play or novel that might have been written, the acting or directing career in the theatre or motion-picture.

Or the odd, sometimes nightmarish atmosphere might stimulate the imagination into viewing the possibilities of making the break into that ever-beckoning monster, television.

Not all of the staff worked on a shift system. Dozens, producers and writers, actors and secretaries, came in every morning at nine-thirty and left every evening at five-thirty, and seldom gave a thought to the others. But the engineers, the announcers, the disk-players, the recording staff, all these were part of a fraternity which had learned to sleep in the daytime, to get up at six o'clock in the evening, have dinner and then come in, by bus or underground train, and walk out of the evening into the artificial lights, the conditioned air of Radio House.

They formed a brotherhood which broadcast, played records, turned control-knobs all the night hours, and then heavy-eyed left again at seven or eight o'clock in the morning, gasping as the chill morning air woke them to the fact of a new day.

Yes, Guy Keaping thought, as he leaned forward, watching the announcer through the control-room window, a man who has worked on a night-shift is different from other men He possesses an awareness of time that other men never acquire. Secretly in his heart he despises, for the rest of his days, the man who sleeps all night, the man who has never kept vigil, in factory, office, or hospital, or broadcasting centre, all through those long, slow hours.

Came the closing announcement. It was a night-recording on account of the difficulty in getting the actor who was playing the murderer, Vaquier, who happened to be filming all day, every day. Next year, Keaping reminded himself, the conceited swine would be out of work for weeks on end. He sighed and eyed the clock.

Thirty seconds and it would be over. Another sample of British justice finished; written, argued about, cast, rehearsed, recorded. Now his work on it was finished. In thirty seconds his creation would be transferred to a spool of magnetized tape. To alter anything he had written would be a surgical operation, carried out with scissors and adhesive tape.

The closing announcement ended. Keaping gave a mutter and the pro-gramme engineer faded out the microphone, called out: 'Grams,' and he faded up the gramophone channel and the closing music came through the loud-speaker. The engineer held it, slowly faded it away. Then he sat back and looked at Keaping.

'They'll never know how close it came

to going up the spout,' Guy Keaping said. 'What did that chump do? Turn over two pages at once?'

The other man nodded. 'I saw him in the pub at closing time, he was knocking a few back.'

'Swine,' Keaping said bitterly. 'Don't care a damn, those people. All they want to do is get it over with and get home.'

The engineer picked up the control phone. 'Recording room? Was it okay? I made the time twenty-eight-thirty.' He listened to the reply, then hung up. 'Says it was okay,' he said to Keaping. 'He'd like to have a word with you about editing, before you go.'

'I'll go along and see him. That's all for to-night. Thanks a lot. You did a good job.'

The engineer looked pleased. Praise was rare. Guy Keaping waved at the actors and actresses in the studio, spoke to them flatteringly, just to leave them happy, and made his way to the recording room at the other end of the corridor. A curly-haired man was putting the spool of tape into its cardboard box, labelling it carefully. 'If you can leave your marked script with me,' he said to Keaping. 'I'll make you an edited version for to-morrow. You want it on disks?'

'On seventy-eights,' Keaping said. He threw his script on to the recording engineer's desk. 'There you are. And you might try and dub out that frightful pause when that bloody moron lost his place.'

The curly-haired man grinned briefly. 'Good job it's on tape,' he said. 'I can cut it right out. You'll never know.'

Keaping looked at the big-faced clock on the wall of the recording-room. He left the other bending over his recording apparatus. Wearily he went along to the canteen. He had reached the stage of fatigue where sleep seems an unimaginable luxury, something once known but long forgotten. He had not slept now for several nights.

He had always had bouts of insomnia at times of worry, anxiety, fear. This was the first for a few months. He had almost forgotten how bad they were, how they turned every waking moment into a nightmare that had somehow to be lived through.

The canteen was nearly empty. The lights burned brightly, coloured fluorescent lights that created an illusion of cheerfulness. They made his eyes ache. Behind the counter the night-staff, phlegmatic middle-aged women, sat talking in low voices. One of them got to her feet and smiled cosily at him. 'What's for you, love?'

'Ham sandwich and coffee please. Strong coffee.'

He had long ago learned that food is a fairly good substitute for sleep. Lack of sleep caused a feeling of nausea, but to accept that nausea and refuse food was fatal. Force yourself to eat, and a certain measure of warmth and alertness returned. He went to an empty table and began to eat the sandwich.

Twenty minutes after eight. Nothing to do until nine-thirty next morning. He dared not go to bed. To lie in bed, sleepless, was the worst kind of punishment he knew. Better to keep going, walk, talk, work, read, anything, until daylight.

Lying down in a dark room, the ghosts began to haunt him, the voices began to sound in his ears. The intolerable accusing voices. The pictures began to form in his brain, pictures he wanted to forget. Her face, blood-splashed. He choked on his sandwich, abruptly he got up from the table, walked out of the canteen.

He reached the hall and almost ran across to the door. He pushed it open and stood on the steps, his breath coming in gasps. From where he stood, he could see the beginning of the Kingsway. He crossed the silent street walked aimlessly up past the Stoll Theatre, then on an impulse he turned right along Sardinia Street. He was alone, with only his shadow and the rhythmic thud-thud of his heels on the pavement for company. This was how he liked London, empty and nostaligc. He walked slowly round Lincolns Inn. A light mist hung along the trees. All around him the ring of offices, houses, solicitors' premises, watched him, with their empty window-eyes.

He was always conscious of being

watched. It was a feeling he had learned to live with, it was a kind of grim companionship. The faces, the eyes, were always accusing. At first he had thought it was impossible to live, with this hanging over him. But he had lived. Living with a bad conscience was like living with a woman you loathe, but to whom you are tied, for life.

His conscience had not grown easier, with the passing of time; grief is dulled by the passage of the years, guilt, Keaping found, festers and turns rotten inside a man.

He turned away from Lincolns Inn, found a devious way through Clements Inn, at the top of Fleet Street, by the Law Courts, and then he crossed Fleet Street and went down Norfolk Street towards the river. He crossed the Embankment and leaned on the smooth, rounded parapet, feeling the grain of the stone under his fingers. He could hear the splash of water, below him, could see the glimmer of lights from the moored vessels away on his left. Wraiths of mist swirled in a sudden night breeze and he caught the unforgettable smell of London river.

He had spent many nights walking about London, in the early days after the horror. He had leaned on this wall and wished bitterly that he had the courage to take a header into the dark water. His head had been full of fearful dreams. Yet it was a hundred-to-one chance that he would ever be connected with the horror of that night.

They had got in to Paris in the early hours. Raoul had lain as if unconscious in the car. When he woke he had complained of a violent headache. He found a gash on his left temple, with dried blood still stuck to it. Astonished he had turned to Keaping.

'*Mon Dieu*, what happened?' he'd said. 'Did we crash?'

'Skidded on a patch of oil. You cracked your head on the windscreen.'

He had hardly been able to speak. In the last few hours he had passed through every emotion of remorse and fear. No other car had come on the scene, no one had seen him kill the girl. He had dropped her passport back on the grass.

got back into the car and driven north as hard as he could.

At first he could barely drive at all, his hands were slippery with sweat, his eyes had kept blurring over with a mist of shock and horror. Raoul had lain in the other seat, breathing stertorously, blood oozing from the cut on his head. He had let him lie there, he had concentrated on putting every mile he could between himself and the girl. He would feel safer, he'd hoped, but fear had clung to him like his shadow.

As he was threading his way through the outskirts of Paris he'd expected at every moment a traffic flic to step out, raise a hand and stop him.

'Where did it happen?' Raoul had asked him. 'The skid I mean?'

'Soon after Lyons. There was a big patch of oil on the road. I didn't spot it in time.' He had practised saying it for hour after hour while he drove.

'Where are you heading for now?'

'Anywhere. Where shall I drop you?'

'A dump in Rue des Saints Peres. Just off St. Germain des Pres. If that's all right with you.'

'That's all right with me.'

Paris was in a pale golden haze of early morning sunshine, but he had no eyes for anything except the street names and the traffic flics. He found the Rue des Saints Peres, pulled up outside the place Raoul pointed out. 'Come in and have a coffee, you look rotten.'

Standing on the pavement Keaping had found his legs were trembling. It was all he could do to get inside the door, which the other held open for him, staring at him curiously. The radio was chattering. A woman had come in, sleepy-eyed and frowsy.

'Can you give us coffee?' Raoul Dassinget said, and she had disappeared into the kitchen. They heard her bustling about.

Then that chattering voice on the radio had suddenly ceased, and a brisker man's voice interrupted. As soon as he began to read the news flash Keaping knew what was coming. He forced himself to sit casually in his chair.

'A tragedy occurred late last night just

north of Lyons. An English girl, apparently a tourist, was knocked down and killed, it is believed by a car travelling north. The girl was identified as Diana Margaret Morse. She received multiple injuries from which she died without regaining consciousness. Her body was discovered by the driver of a long-distance camion. Whoever knocked her down has so far not reported the accident to the police.'

Raoul Dassinget had become like a man demented. 'It's Diana. She's been killed. Run over by some swine who wouldn't stop.'

Guy Keaping hadn't been able to stand any more. The café was warm, but he had begun to shiver. There was bile in his mouth. The voice on the radio and Dassinget's voice came and went in his ears. He staggered to the door and out into the street. There he was violently sick.

When he pulled himself upright and wiped his bitter mouth with his hand he saw Dassinget standing in the café doorway. Then slowly he had come over to him. 'It was you,' he said.

18

He was going back to this Radio House job. The security of his aunt's legacy. Then this first nightmare. Guy Keaping drew a long, shuddering breath at the memory of it. He moved along the Embankment towards Waterloo Bridge. The benches were empty. Only on one a huddled figure stirred under a heap of newspapers and muttered something as he passed, scuffing at the damp yellow leaves underfoot. They were beginning to fall, now. The Indian summer was nearly over.

Ahead of him, the necklace of lights that was Waterloo Bridge, glittered in the darkness. The breeze was stiffening, and as he saw the black outline of the police station beside the river, he reflected grimly how two years ago, he would have crossed the road, but now he walked past it unmoved, only his hand clenching. On towards Charing Cross, his feet moving automatically.

On these long night-walks he set an automatic pilot in his brain, and his feet obeyed. He never consciously chose a route, though after he could not remember where he had walked during the night. Now, his thoughts in France, his feet took him up Villiers Street towards Charing Cross Station. He heard nothing of the noise of the trains, the shunting, clanking noise of a railway at night. He was like a man sleeping.

Then, the second nightmare. That first accusation, when after staggering out of the café, vomiting on the pavement, he had faced Raoul and his: '*It was you.*'

The coincidence of Dassinget's head-injury, the skid Keaping had admitted, his nausea at the account of the accident, it had been enough to make the other jump to the conclusion that it was the M.G. which had killed Diana.

'What do you care?' Keaping had said. 'You'd left her two hundred miles from Paris and you'd filled yourself with booze.'

Raoul had lit a Gaullois with unsteady

hands. His eyes, feverishly bright, were searching Keaping's face. Then, almost amiably: 'You'd better tell me how it happened.'

They had gone back into the café. They had faced each other across the table with the checked tablecloth and the café noise, and he had recalled what had happened.

'You were drunk,' he had said, stubbornly, as though in some way it had been responsible for the whole thing. 'Soon after we left Lyons you went off into a stupor. I drove for a long time. I kept a look-out for your girl, but there was no one who looked like her. After a while I forgot about her and just drove.'

His hands had been shaking so that the coffee slopped in his saucer. 'I was going at a fair speed, then suddenly she jumped up, right in front of the car, waving like mad, trying to flag me down. I hadn't a chance. I swerved, pulled the wheel over, skidded. I ran back. She was by the side of the road. She'd been thrown some distance. She was dead.'

What had come over him? What dreadful fear had taken possession of his heart and mind? There was his bad driving-record in Engand of course. Drunkenness, dangerous driving, it wouldn't have looked too good. That and his new job, and the money waiting for him, which was going to build him a new life. A new beginning. This would have ruined it. This damned girl, a stranger, who'd stepped into the path of his car. And he was half-boozed, that would have stuck out a mile to the flics.

But it had gone deeper than that. Some inexplicable dread had gripped him, some submerged animal fear had welled up and urged him to run for it. To shrink from any responsibility for what he had done. And then it had to be Dassinget's girl, it had to be her.

Dassinget hadn't told him the girl's name, only what she looked like and a few dirty innuendos about the poor kid. Would it have made any difference, if he had realized who she was? He couldn't have answered that. It hadn't mattered. Dassinget had hardly said a word of regret about her. In fact, he might have been quite happy, the way it had worked out for him. Only Keaping hadn't thought of that in the café. 'An empty road, at night,' he said. 'That M.G. You couldn't expect I'd be creeping along at thirty.'

'And you were half-sozzled,' Dassinget had said. 'All that wine.'

Keaping had looked away, silently.

'I suggest you forget the whole ghastly business,' Dassinget had said. 'I wouldn't dream of turning you in,' with a sudden grin.

He said he knew where he could dispose of the car, no questions asked. Keaping had left it with him. That morning he had caught a plane back to London. Dassinget was staying behind in Paris for a few days.

As the plane droned over the Channel, Keaping had sat staring out, re-living time and time again the terrible moment when the girl jumped up in front of his car. He would never forget the sight of her, crumpled, blood-spattered, twisted, by the road.

Dassinget had bade him an almost too casual good-bye. 'I'll look out for you.'

244

And then he'd said: 'I'm at Radio House. French broadcasts.' He had smiled at Keaping. 'If I hear anything about what happened, I'll let you know.' He might have been referring to an incident of the most trivial importance. 'I don't suppose there'd be much about it in the papers.'

Now, Guy Keaping found himself outside Charing Cross Station, staring unseeingly at the garish street-lamps of the Strand. He made his way to Trafalgar Square, crossed the road and went down the steps towards the fountains. Trafalgar Square, vulgar and noisy by day, was almost deserted, a few figures passed the looming shapes of the lions, the basins of the fountains were smooth and cold to the touch.

He sat down, his legs a little weak with weariness, and he blinked heavy lids and stared ahead, his mind alive with pictures of the past.

The second nightmare had started soon after Dassinget's return to London. Keaping had asked him how much he'd got for the M.G. Not much, the other had told him, his tone coolly casual. Keaping, stung by Dassinget's calculated evasiveness, had pressed him. The reply had been terse, brutal and straight to the point. 'I'm hanging on to it, anyway, so why should it trouble you how much?'

Incensed, Keaping had started to protest vigorously but the other had interrupted him with a sneer. 'I'm sure my silence is worth that small sum of money to you?'

'What d'you mean, your silence?'

'You know very well what I mean.' Dassinget's eyes had narrowed with hatred. 'You killed Diana and you got away with it. If you want to stay that way, you'd better make it worth my while.'

And from that demand had sprung others. Sickened, frightened, Guy Keaping could do nothing but pay. The legacy his aunt had left him had been dissipated with terrifying rapidity. But now, now it had ended.

Unable yet to comprehend it, he sat there in the cool glimmer of Trafalgar Square, the long nightmare over. He found himself clenching and unclenching his right fist, and stopped, sweat moistening his brow.

Now, he thought, his tired brain working slowly, I can start again. I still have my job. I can start to build up again; and this time on good foundations. Or was it already too late? Could one go on making fresh starts, time after time? Hadn't he failed too often in the past? He stood up and moved on, his mind churning. His life had been a succession of failures. Could a man recover from all this and more, and yet make something of himself?

Along Pall Mall he proceeded, up the Haymarket, to Piccadilly Circus, oblivious of the thinning traffic and people. The breeze that had begun as a breath over the river was stronger now, as he found himself walking faster. Oxford Circus, Cavendish Square. Faster he walked, his eyes brighter than they had been for a long time, his limbs moving with new energy. The sky was dark, cloudy. A thin slice of moon rode behind the clouds.

Opposite 221b Harley Street, he came to a standstill. From the pavement across the street he looked up at the dark windows. He stood for a long time in the quiet street, staring across at the house.

He was just turning away, indecisively, when he jerked his head round. The door of 221b was opening.

19

Miss Frayle lay in bed looking across at the windows from which the curtains were drawn, her bedside-lamp was switched off but the room was light enough from the tall street-lamps. It was really autumn now, she was thinking, and she sighed regretfully. She had no liking for the darkening days of the end of the year.

She felt overcome with an acute depression which could not be attributed to the effects of the blow on the head. She had awoken about a quarter-of-an-hour ago, her headache completely gone. The travelling-clock on the bedside-table said that it was just on nine o'clock. She wondered where Dr. Morelle was, working in the study, as usual, no doubt. Had there been any developments about the Carla Collins business? Her mind unwound back to the party at the house in Little Venice.

Looking back now upon the events following the discovery of the girl's death, her thoughts circled round the incident when Bill Scott had told her he knew who'd killed her. She reflected that since Inspector Hood had acted upon her reference to this, there had been nothing to it. Bill Scott had been lying to her, trying to throw suspicion upon Dassinget, of course. A wave of restlessness surged through her. She threw back the bedclothes, pulled on her dressing-gown and crossed to the window.

The night-sky was clear beyond the roof-tops. She heard a solitary car purr along the street below; a train gave a whistle from Marylebone Station. Far away she thought she caught the mournful note of a ship's siren, carried on the night beeze.

As she heard the nostalgic sounds she felt a longing for some sort of action, something to do. A reaction to her enforced idleness for the past several hours. Her thoughts focussed on Radio House and the hum of suppressed excitement that pervaded the atmosphere of the place. She supposed it had got into her blood a little, the odd glamour of radio, a dying business though it might be.

Images of Doug Blackwood flitted across her mind, and Betty Lewis, plain-featured and intense. She sighed again as she thought how foolish the girl was to give rein to her infatuation for Raoul Dassinget. And there was Guy Keaping, burdened, she was convinced, with some secret sorrow. It seemed strange that she might never see him again, and a pang stabbed her heart. There was something about him which attracted her. No doubt about that.

Resolutely she thrust the picture of those heavy features and lean frame out of her mind, and began wondering about herself. Herself and her job. Her job here, with Dr. Morelle. Was she really dissatisfied with it? She had left it before to go to other jobs, and she had come back and been glad to. More thankful than she had ever let Dr. Morelle realize.

Or had he guessed, she reflected ruefully, all the time, which was why he knew that sooner or later she would return to him? But this was different, this time, she felt sure. During her short stay at Radio House, she had heard many young women say they could never work anywhere else, even though the pay was not high. Now she thought she under-stood. She had spent only a few weeks there and here she was telling herself she would have to make up her mind what to do.

The prospect of telling Dr. Morelle that she was thinking of leaving him, of trying to land a job at Radio House filled her with not a little trepidation. She gave a sudden start. Was that a knock at the door? Was it Dr. Morelle inquiring after her headache? She went hastily across and opened it. There was no one.

As she stood there, she amused herself by giving her imagination full play. Supposing it had been Dr. Morelle, tall, dark, sombre-faced, with some flowers for her? Or a box of chocolates, or even just a kind word would have been enough. She closed the door on the empty darkness and the fleeting picture her mind had conjured up, she knew he was in his study, or the laboratory without pausing in his work to think about her or how she was feeling.

All the same, as she went back to the bedroom, she was conscious of a horrid feeling of disloyalty. She was thinking of leaving him, working out how best to tell him, and he was blissfully unconscious of it.

Again the longing for some activity possessed her. She glanced out of the window. A brisk walk round the houses, perhaps up Portland Place as far as Regent's Park, was what she would enjoy. That's what she'd do. She switched on the light and hurriedly put on some clothes.

A glance at the travelling-clock told her it was seven minutes past nine. She slipped out of her flat quietly and down the stairs. She paused in the hall and looked back at the study. There was no sound, but she thought she could detect a faint thin glow indicative of a light burning behind the closed study-door. He was there, she decided. Again she hesitated, and then moved to the front door.

As she closed the door behind her and went down the steps, she clutched her coat collar under her chin. Autumn was round the corner all right, there was a decided nip in the air.

And then the figure was crossing the street towards her.

'Hello, Miss Frayle.'

For a moment she thought she must be dreaming. She stood there, unable to say anything. Guy Keaping smiled down at her as casually and self-assured as if they were at his office in Radio House.

'I was just going for a walk,' was all she could think of.

'Me, too,' he said. 'Let's go together.'

His hand took her arm and as if in a trance she walked beside him. He chatted to her quietly, telling her that he'd been working late and afterwards had felt the need for some exercise and air, as she had herself, and that quite by chance his footsteps had led him to Harley Street.

Guy Keaping made it sound convincing enough, he did not tell her of the long tortuous journey he had taken into the past while he had walked the pavements; nor did he refer to the compulsion which had urged him to choose the direction he had.

He expressed his surprised pleasure at this unexpected encounter with her which had resulted from his wandering in the night. He skimmed over the little matter of the force which had drawn him to this part of London. She recalled that he lived in Bayswater.

'Yes,' he said. 'But I couldn't face up to going straight home to-night.' He spoke lightly. She glanced up at him, her eyes behind her horn-rims clouded a little in perplexity. She still felt like pinching herself to make sure she really was awake.

He had steered her along Devonshire Street in the direction of Portland Street, where she had mentioned to him, she had intended to go.

'The house I live in,' he was saying, 'harbours a pretty collection of people. Old trouts who've come down in the world, the kind who did their shopping at Harrods once, and now creep shame-facedly into Woolworths; who go to seances and spiritualist meetings, or who patronize dingy little club theatres. And of course, there's me.'

He fell silent and they went on together, Miss Frayle saying nothing either, vaguely regretting that she had come out, that she would have been better off back in bed. But then she hadn't known that she was going to find Guy Keaping waiting for her, practically on the doorstep.

A vision floated before her of the house where he lived. A big house, with basement-windows peering over the edge of the pavement, and within, a large, dingy entrance-hall, with flaking paint and huge dim oil-paintings high up on the walls. She had once lived in a house like that, and she gave him a look.

For a moment she fancied it had been on the tip of his tongue to invite her along, and she had another vision of the sort of room his would be. Shabby and decayed. But he didn't ask her.

Instead he said: 'Have you heard about

Dassinget?' When she looked up at him questioningly, he told her, and she gave such a gasp of horror that he stopped and took her arm to steady her. Her hands fluttered helplessly, as he told her more about it. She felt sure she could hear a note of thankfulness in his voice. He trailed off and she looked at him curiously, he had been telling her about Dr. Morelle's visit to Radio House shortly before Dassinget's death.

'What is it?' she said.

'You see,' he said, 'though why you should be interested, I can't imagine — ' he still hesitated. 'I'd met him in France, I'd had news about an aunt, she'd just died and left me some money.' His face was suddenly bitter in the light of a street lamp. 'I'd been in Marseilles and driving back to Paris. Fast as I could make it. On the way I stopped at Lyons. It was there I met Dassinget. He'd just ditched his girl-friend. He had a bad conscience, but not bad enough. I drove him back to Paris. I had a hope we might pick his girl up on the road.'

They were in Portland Place, heading

for the top of it, where a shadow of trees stood stark against the sky. 'He went to sleep,' he said hoarsely, his words gathered momentum. 'I was driving fast, it was night, as I said, and suddenly a girl jumped up in front of the car. I hit her. Dassinget was knocked-out, when I braked. I got out and looked at the girl. She was dead. It was the one he'd behaved so badly to. She'd obviously started to hitch-hike back to Paris. I got back into the car and drove on.'

She stared at him. She was still feeling shocked by the news of Dassinget's death. She knew it was murder, it was obvious from the way Guy Keaping had told it to her, that it wasn't accidental death. 'You mustn't blame yourself,' she heard herself say. This was the secret sorrow she had known instinctively had borne him down? Or was there more to come?

He laughed abruptly. 'That was only the beginning. He blackmailed me.'

So that was what it was. She clutched her coat-collar again, a chill wind sped down Portland Place from the park. What could she say to him now?

And then as she opend her mouth to murmur something commiserating, the full impact of what he had told her struck her. He had turned and faced her. His eyes were strained, desperate. 'If the police find out about the blackmail, they'll pin it on me.'

'But you must be able to prove that you didn't — '

'Just before he was killed,' he said grimly, 'I went along to his office. As I came out, I saw Bill Scott waiting outside. He'd said he was going to see him about the Collins girl.'

'Then that proves he was alive when you left him.'

'Only Bill Scott denies going in. He says he didn't go into Dassinget's office at all.' He stared at Miss Frayle. 'What do you suppose they'd do about that? Toss for it?'

Her eyes searching his haggard face, her thoughts raced back to Dr. Morelle. It was on the tip of her tongue to tell Guy Keaping that he must go back with her now, he must tell all that he'd told her to Dr. Morelle. And then black doubt assailed her.

This man she thought she knew a little and for whom she felt a definite attraction, felt a certain affection, what was he? He had killed a girl in his car and left her and driven off. He had allowed himself to be blackmailed. All this he had confessed to her. Had he been hanging about outside 221b Harley Street, trying to work up enough courage to see Dr. Morelle? To confess to him even more than he had confessed to her?

'And as if I haven't told you enough about myself,' he was saying bitterly, and she saw that his face was stiff, so that his lips barely moved as he went on, 'to make you realize the sort of swine I am, there's something else.'

She caught her breath. This was it. This was the other thing that he had been spurring himself to tell Dr. Morelle as he'd waited outside the house. She was trembling, she could feel her knees weaken while she waited for him to continue, waited and yet wished that he would stop now, and let her return to the safety of Harley Street, without hearing any more.

'It's about what happened this afternoon,' he said, remorselessly, 'at Grove Mansions. What happened to you. Oh yes,' he said as her eyes widened, 'I know all about it. That's what I've got to tell you.'

He had taken her arm again and was urging her along beside him as if he needed to continue walking in order to help him shift the burden of guilt that was weighing him down. She suddenly saw that they had turned off Portland Place and were already along a side-street a few yards. In her moment of rising panic she couldn't tell the name of the street they were in.

She only knew it was completely deserted, and as they approached a dark patch before the next street-lamp, she heard with a sudden chill at her heart the squeak-squeak of the shoes of the man beside her.

20

Bill Scott had made his way home through the rush-hour crowds, seeing none of the business-girls chattering like sparrows as they hurried along the Strand towards Charing Cross. He had looked in none of the lighted shop-windows, never once glanced up to the darkening sky above his head; he heard nothing of the roar of traffic.

Bill Scott had been possessed of only one idea, to get back to his bed-sitting-room, to shut the door behind him, and then to force his courage to that irrevocable decision.

It was a long way to his home, but he wanted to walk, he wanted to avoid the curious gazes of fellow bus-passengers. He walked quickly. London is the best place in which to be unhappy, suddenly Bill Scott remembered the words. Someone had used them, was it in a programme? The best place to be unhappy, because the age-old patience of its stones soaks up, absorbs mere small and personal miseries. Touch the river wall with your hands and feel the strength of stone seep into you. Know that hundreds of others have stood looking into the water, unhappy, desperate. Know you are not alone.

Alone, a solitary man, man with a heart squeezed dry of hope. He walked on through the fast-falling night. A car hooted furiously as he made to step blindly into the road. A taxi-driver leaned out and cursed him. He did not hear. Across the road, round a corner, and another.

It was quite dark when he let himself into the house, and slowly climbed the stairs to his room. He met no one. People kept strange hours in this house, he seldom saw them. Another key. Then he was in his familiar room. He switched on the light and pushed the door shut behind him and stood there, his eyes dry and burning, his face lined.

The inevitable radio by his divan bed. Books everywhere. The coffee-table, his gaze moved slowly round the room. It went up to a picture on the wall. By some trick of the light it seemed to be her face that stared at him out from the frame.

He gave a sob that choked in his throat. He looked wildly about him, at the window, the door. It was a small room, the window looking down onto the street was open a few inches at the top. He closed it. Then he held his hand to where the latch held the windows together. After a moment he nodded to himself.

He drew the heavy, old and musty curtains. He examined the cracks at the bottom of the door. He stooped and pushed the bedside rug hard up against the door. He looked round again.

No air through the window. The door was all right. Satisfied, he bent down again and with a hand that shook a little he turned on the gas-fire tap.

He realized for the first time that he was still wearing his outdoor coat. He slipped it off and threw it on the divan. Then he took a cushion and laid it on the floor in front of the gas fire. He looked at it uncertainly, then dragged the top blanket from the divan. He arranged it on the floor, as carefully as if he were making it up as a bed.

The smell of the hissing gas was already noticeable. It was unpleasant and he suddenly turned away and went across to the window. Pulling aside the heavy velvet curtain he stood staring out across the street.

The last time, he thought. His last look at London. Dark, chill, yet with its muted traffic friendly sounds that came across the square. London had meant a lot to him. It had been his home. He had worked here, loved here. Laughed once, a long time ago. But not for a long time. Not since it had happened.

He let the curtain fall back into place, shutting out the night, and went back across the room and lay down in front of the gas fire, pulling the blanket up over him. He had not realized how tired he was. The smell of gas was bad.

His mind jarred back into its inevitable groove. She was dead. The nightmare ought to have stopped, after Dassinget's death. It ought to have closed the chapter.

It ought to be possible now to forget, to push the whole thing into the past.

Instead, fear had been added to his misery. Everyone knew how he'd hated Dassinget. Of course they would suspect him.

How could all this have happened to me? he asked himself. How have I got involved in all this misery, this tragedy? All I wanted was an ordinary, fairly happy life. I didn't ask for anything much. Just a fair measure of fun. And it's all turned sour on me; hopeless, miserable, I've taken this as the only way out.

The gas was making him feel light-headed, drowsy. He closed his eyes and found it difficult to believe that he could even lift his heavy eye-lids again. The floor was hard under his back.

He thought he heard footsteps ascending the stairs. One of the other tenants coming home from work probably. They were an odd lot, a typical cross-section for a programme about a London apartment-house, he thought drowsily. Couple of middle-aged suspicious Viennese, an elderly spinster living on twopence ha'penny, and two or three men like himself, men without roots, men who lived out their lives in tatty London third-floor, shabby rooms.

How many of them finish like this, he wondered? Lying in front of a gas fire with the tap turned full on?

His thoughts were drifting, hovering just out of reach. Faces and shapes loomed up at him and dissolved. It was like falling to sleep. There was nothing to it. You lie there trying to think about a particular thing and it eludes you. You know if you make an effort, even move a limb, you'll wake up enough to catch the thought. Only you can't make the effort. You try, feebly, and let it go; and sleep comes down like a heavy blanket, shutting you off. This time, though, he thought absently, it would be shutting him off from everything forever.

The heavy-jawed face of Inspector Hood swam up before him, pipe jutting out from under the grizzled moustache. Once again he was answering questions, each question which seemed to start in a whisper and then grow increasingly louder, before it exploded in his ears. The fool, as if he would kill Carla Collins. Couldn't the man who kept asking him stupid, meaningless things see that he loved her?

Dassinget, his thoughts drifted off again, the sweetish smell of the gas becoming more sickly, Dassinget, that was different. And now the Frenchman's face swam out of the mist, as the gas hissed louder and louder in his ears. Dassinget, who had gone the way of Carla.

He could hear his own voice now, answering the Scotland Yard man: '*Yes, I went to his office, to knock the living daylights out of him. I know he killed Carla.*' And the big man, Inspector Hood, eyeing him calmly over his pipe.

Now other voices rose up at him, no shutting his ears to them. Scornful, derisive voices, and there were distorted faces. And always her face among them.

He was breathing stertorously. His eyes were shut, his face white. Under the blanket his hands twitched as he hovered between life and death. Outside the evening had darkened into night. Lights gleamed in the square, showing up the yellowing leaves of the tall trees. People walked fast, eager to shut their doors behind them and enter into the comfort of their homes.

A taxi pulled up outside the house. The driver looked at the coin that gleamed in the light from his meter, grinned at his fare, and drove away. The front door opened and shut noisily. Footsteps hurrying up the stairs, on to his landing and up again, to the top of the house.

Inside the room, the gas hissed, a steady insistent sound. Bill Scott muttered something and turned restlessly, clutching at the blanket.

The haunting faces, the voices, were fading now. It was like floating, not very high, but just above the surface of the ground. A feeling of lightness, of freedom. Nothing could touch him now. It was a long time since he had known real peace. He hovered, aware only of the small fear that this sensation would not last, that the nightmare would return.

But this was more final than sleep.

21

In the train bearing her homewards, Betty Lewis had sat hunched in a corner of the compartment, Doug Blackwood's words chasing round her brain. He had talked to her all the way to Victoria in the taxi after their encounter with Dr. Morelle. Her face still burned at the recollection of what he'd told her.

'You were lonely,' he said. 'No man had ever taken the trouble to make a pass at you, and you were afraid you'd missed the boat. You wanted a lover, and you didn't give a damn what kind of man he was, so long as he was yours. And so when that rat made up to you, you threw yourself at him.'

Each word hitting her like a blow, she had tried to silence him but he had continued inexorably. 'You wouldn't have lasted long. A month or two. Perhaps less. Then he'd have dropped you. And that would have been bad. You'd have wanted to kill yourself, or you'd have wanted to do him.'

It was when he had compared her with Bill Scott that she had smacked his face, only for him to grin at her. 'Got you on the raw, eh?' he said. 'But that's how he's reacted to Carla's sticky end. Brimming over with self-pity. Why you and he don't get together, I wouldn't know.'

He had watched her from the taxi, still with that mocking grin, and she had looked back from the crowd milling into the station. He had waved to her and then the taxi-door had slammed on his big, strong figure and he had been driven off. Back to his house at Little Venice, she supposed.

As the train had pulled out, her mind had gone back to the party the night before, and Bill Scott, when he'd rushed in with the news that he'd found Carla Collins. His thin, hollow-cheeked, deathly white features, and popping eyes, his mouth working convulsively.

He had loved her. Death had robbed him, as it had her. Doug Blackwood had been right, they were both in the same boat. A sudden, sickening emotion gripped her. It was as if a lightning-flash had split the darkness of her mind, darkness which had obscured every rational thought. The darkness of despair over Dassinget's end which had numbed her faculties.

But now the lightning-flash dispersed the blackness and showed her the step she must take, the action she must follow. The removal of Dassinget from the scene made that which had not been possible before, possible now, imperative even.

Two of the passengers who occupied the half-full compartments stood up, reaching for their bowler-hats and umbrellas. The train was drawing into the first stop after leaving Victoria and her mind made up there and then Betty Lewis got out. She saw that a train back to Victoria was running into the next platform and she dashed over the foot-bridge. She was just in time to throw herself into an empty compartment.

Her first thoughts as she began to reason more clearly had been to go straight to Dr. Morelle. Then as her determination was followed by action, another idea struck her. Perhaps her first move lay in another direction? Arrived at Victoria again, she was filled with a sudden intuition that speed was necessary to her new resolve, she got a taxi and told the driver to make it snappy.

The square was gloomy, and although she knew the address, she had a good head for addresses and telephone-numbers, she hadn't been there before. The taxi prowled round searching for the number of the house. At last she saw it, and got out, paid off the taxi, and she hurried up the front steps.

A man, for a moment, she thought it was the one she was seeking, was going in. She called after him and he turned and when she saw it was a stranger, she asked him to leave the door open, she was expected, she said glibly.

There was a list of names on a wooden board nailed up inside the dimly-lit hall. A. Rosenbaum. Z. Paimovich. Miss H. Goodbody. J. Adeney. Then she saw the name she wanted.

She went upstairs, saw the door and

knocked, and waited. No sound from inside. She suddenly realized that he mightn't be in. There was no reason why he should be. He wasn't expecting her. She was the last person.

She saw the key in the lock. She knocked again, louder, and waited, but still there was no sound. Irritated at the thought of having come on a wild-goose chase, she turned the key. She pushed the door open with difficulty, and the gas hit her.

At once she knew what had happened. Pushing with all her strength, she opened the door wide, reeled back, coughing and saw him at once, lying on the floor in front of the fire. The room was full of gas. Burying her face in her arms, she crossed to the window and tugged at the curtains. The gas made her cough. Tears sprang to her eyes. She unfastened the catch, pushed the bottom half of the window as far up as it would go, and leaned her head out, gulping in great breaths of air.

She turned back to where Bill Scott lay. She turned off the gas-tap. The sinister hissing stopped abruptly. A draught blew between the open window and the door, wedged open by the rolled-up carpet in which it was caught. Bill Scott lay white and still.

She started to pull him across the floor, out into the passage. The gas fumes swirled about her and she wanted to be sick. She didn't call out, instead she rolled the inert body over on to its face, turned the head to one side, pulled his jacket off. Then she knelt down by his head, took hold of his arms and began a rhythmical count.

The thing she had learned to do at first-aid classes. The thing she had never expected to do in real life. No grinning mock-patient, this. All the time she watched Bill Scott's face, watched for the faintest flicker of the closed eyelids, the slightest gasp for air. She had nearly given up hope when his eyes quivered, half opened, then closed again. He gave a weak groan.

'It's Betty Lewis,' she said. 'Breathe in all the air you can. Breathe.'

He was trying to do what she told him. To breathe deeply, strongly. No one from any of the other rooms seemed to have heard a thing. There wasn't a sound from upstairs or below. He rolled over on his back, struggling from her grip and stared up at her, at first without comprehension. Then he started to frown at her.

'You bloody fool,' she said quietly. 'Why did you try and do it?'

His face creased into an expression of acute distress and he put an arm over his eyes. She saw that he was crying. Compassionately she put her arms under his shoulders and tried to raise him. 'I'll help you up.'

Together they staggered across to the room and he half-fell into a chair. The gas was blowing out of the windows and into the house. She heard the sounds of movement above, someone asked in a foreign accent if there was a gas-leak. She called upstairs that it was all right, and shut the door. Bill Scott's face was ghastly, he was weeping silently. 'Not to worry,' she said brightly. 'It'll be all right.'

He didn't answer, he was quite unable to speak. She found milk and an electric kettle, and set about making some tea. A few minutes later she had two cups of strong, scalding tea, very sweet. 'Knock it back,' she said. 'It'll take that filthy taste away.'

He took the cup with shaking hands and gulped the tea. It was so hot that he choked and gasped. Slowly he drank it in sips. When he had emptied the cup a little colour had returned to his face. She poured him another cup.

He looked bitterly at the girl. 'Why did you have to come in and stop me?' he said, hoarsely. 'I don't want to live.'

'Of course you do,' she said briskly. 'By this time tomorrow, you'll be thanking your lucky stars I turned up like I did. In the nick of time.'

He moved his head from side to side, wearily as if trying to brush her words away. But she went on talking. 'You're not the only one with trouble, you know. But they don't all turn the gas on to sneak out of them.'

He looked at her with naked hostility. 'You don't understand. You and Dassinget, that's different. He deserved what he got. He murdered Carla. Oh, I know it can't be proved, but he did it.'

Her face had become tight, withdrawn. 'Yes, it was Raoul,' she said quietly. 'That's what I came to tell you. It doesn't matter now, and I thought you should know the truth. I'm going to tell Dr. Morelle and the police.'

He stared at her with hollow eyes. 'You knew? But you shielded him.'

'Carla was nothing to me,' she said. 'He was everything.' Her voice shook.

'But why did he kill her?'

She shook her head dumbly. 'He didn't mean to, he swore he didn't mean to. They quarrelled over — over something, I don't know what it was — and he hit her with a wine-bottle. He panicked and pushed her into the pond, to make it look as if she'd drowned herself.'

Abruptly he got up from the chair and stumbled across to the wide-open window. A breeze was flapping the heavy curtains. She could see he was shivering all over, his hands were clasped tightly together. He turned to her, as if to ask her what was next to be done. What could anyone do now? he seemed to be asking her.

'Killing yourself won't help,' she said. 'People like you and I have got to go on living.'

'Then who killed him?' he said slowly.

She didn't answer. She finished her tea, eyeing him over the rim of her cup. From a street beyond the square a car hooted irritably. The world was still spinning round, life was still carrying on. Thousands, millions of people were thinking it worth while to go on with the job of living. She caught sight of herself in the mirror over the fireplace. What she saw made her grimace. Dull tangly hair, dingy skin, haphazard make-up. She was about to take her make-up case out of her handbag, instead she decided to leave it until she was out of this house.

'I can tell you one thing,' he said, 'for sure. I didn't push him. I wish I had, I wish I had done the swine in.'

She stood up quickly. She moved across to the door, her back to it, she reached for the handle. Her eyes never left him. He came towards her. 'You know,' he said. 'You know.'

He was grim and white, his eyes sunk deep in his emaciated face. His hands twitched. She opened the door. She started to say something, then she changed her mind.

She slammed the door behind her, and he heard her hurrying footsteps down the stairs.

22

Miss Frayle stopped in her tracks. Never had she felt so cut-off from the world as she felt now, in that quiet street where the tall lamps threw down their pools of light contrasting so sharply with the patches of blackness in between. A patch of blackness in which she and the man beside her had paused.

Even though they had halted the squeak-squeak of his shoes still echoed hideously on the night air, the houses about her continued to throw the sound back at her.

She threw a quick glance behind her. There lay Portland Place some thirty yards away, and a car went past quietly and swiftly, otherwise it seemed quite deserted. She turned and looked ahead. Two or three parked cars glimmered in the shadows but no sign of any human being, not a soul about.

It was then that she noticed, a few

yards ahead on her left, the entrance to a mews. They had been approaching it, and she thought as icy fingers closed more tightly round her heart, what an ideal place it would make to drag her and deal with her as he had done before.

Only this time he would finish the job.

Involuntarily she started to cry out, but her throat was so dry with fright, only a faint groan escaped. But the sound brought his face sharply round to her. It was as if he had only just realized that they had stopped walking.

'Are you all right, Miss Frayle?' He sounded concerned. 'You're shivering.'

'I am a bit cold. I expect it's coming out after being in the warm.' He was looking at her curiously, and she was terrified he'd realized she had guessed the truth about him. 'I — I think I'll turn back,' she managed to say.

'Come on, then,' he said. 'I'll take your arm.'

He linked his arm through hers and they turned and retraced their steps. The squeak-squeak sounded clamorously in her ears; that, together with the pounding of her heart, seemed to fill the universe.

Her thoughts were spinning round. It seemed incredible, yet she knew it was true, he fitted in so perfectly. He had been there at Grove Mansions, to try and stop her, he said, from seeing Raoul Dassinget. He had tried to warn her off. *'Are you hoping to trap him into confessing he murdered Carla?'* That was what he had said to her, and she recalled the under-current of violence in his tone. *'How naïve can you get?'*

She had been naïve all right, she told herself now. Believing in him, the way she had. Thinking he'd tried to stop her from seeing Dassinget for her safety's sake.

It was obvious to her now, of course, he'd simply waited until she had gone inside Grove Mansions, and then he had hurried in after her, followed her by way of the stairs. When she had gone alone to the flat, he could have turned into the other passage and called her, disguising his voice by mimicing Dassinget.

And when she went along towards the emergency stairs, he was waiting in the dark. Waiting to strike.

But why, she asked herself, why? To stop her going to see Dassinget at all costs. Yes, that was plain enough. To stop her finding out that Dassinget was blackmailing him? Could that be the reason? Because he planned to kill Dassinget and didn't want it known for obvious reasons that he was under the Frenchman's thumb.

Squeak-squeak went his shoes, just as they had sounded when she had heard them at Grove Mansions.

She became aware of a voice beside her and realized he had been talking to her all the time they were walking back, she supposed she must have made automatically appropriate replies.

She glanced up at him and was sure she detected an unusual glint in his gaze as he turned his head to her. Then he looked ahead. They were approaching Harley Street, and her heart leapt with thankfulness. A policeman on his beat was passing slowly down the street, a taxi drew up outside a house and two people got out, a car purred comfortingly past. Suddenly the world which had seemed deserted and full of deathly fear, was alive and normal and serene.

Miss Frayle felt safe again. She was within a stone's throw of 221b Harley Street, where Dr. Morelle would be working quietly, and to whom she would in a few moments be unfolding her terrific news. It would be dynamite, she told herself.

'Been a very pleasant little stroll, Miss Frayle.' Once more she shot a look into his face, as he glanced down at her. A great pang smote her. This was the man she had felt affectionate towards, fond of, even. This was the man she had believed reciprocated her somewhat tender feelings. She gulped painfully. It seemed incredible that she could have been so mistaken in him. She tried to read in his face that she was completely wrong, that he was not what she now knew him to be.

But all she saw was a faint smile, a wistful smile, perhaps, as he said: 'I'll be pushing along on my way home, I think.'

'All right,' she said, quickly. 'Shall — shall I tell Dr. Morelle what you've told me?'

He stood there, the heavily-chiselled lines of his face softened by the shadows. 'If you think he'd be interested,' he said lightly. 'Or,' and he grinned at her openly, 'if he doesn't know already.'

It flashed across her mind that his appearance in Harley Street had not been accidental at all. She was suddenly convinced that he had arrived deliberately intent on bringing her out of the house under some pretext with the object of silencing her. And then, she wondered, why if that had been his object, why should she spell danger to him?

She couldn't grasp it. Unless Dassinget's death had in some way altered circumstances for Guy Keaping. And yet how could that be?

It struck her with terrific force. It could be, it could fit in, if he had killed Dassinget. Involuntarily her hand flew to her mouth. Was that it? She was unknowingly in possession of something, some knowledge which linked him with the Frenchman's death, the death of the very creature who had been blackmailing him.

Again his solicitous voice.

'Are you all right, Miss Frayle?'

Again, his sympathetic look, his move towards her, as if his only concern was for her well-being. She managed to save herself from drawing back. 'I — I'm quite all right, really,' she said. 'It's just a bit chilly, that's all.'

'Better get along in, then. Good night, perhaps I'll be hearing from you — or Dr. Morelle — in due course.'

He turned abruptly away, before she could answer him, so that she was reminded of the time before outside Grove Mansions. He had left her then sharply, almost angrily. Only he had come after her, behind her back.

The thought made her spin on her heels and run the rest of the way along Harley Street, only stopping when she was a few yards away from 221b, and she saw someone come out and walk quickly away in the opposite direction. Incredulously she stared after the hurrying figure.

It was Betty Lewis.

There was no mistaking it, and Miss Frayle made as if to call after her. Then decided against it, Dr. Morelle could explain the girl's presence, no doubt, as well as she could herself. Remembering Betty Lewis's exhibitionistic infatuation for Raoul Dassinget, Miss Frayle decided her visit to 221b Harley Street would be concerned with his death, his murder, as Guy Keaping inferred to her that it was.

Her head a confusion of ideas and speculations, Miss Frayle let herself into the house, and made her way straight to the study. Dr. Morelle was at his desk, poring over some papers, his gaunt features looking as if they were carved from ivory in the light from his desk-lamp.

He didn't look up as she went in, closing the door behind her.

'It would appear you are feeling somewhat recovered from your accident,' he said, his gaze still bent over the desk and scribbling a note in the margin of a paper from a folder. 'I'm so glad.'

She ignored what she felt was the mistakably sarcastic edge to his tone, so anxious was she to learn what Betty Lewis had been telling him. 'I just missed

Betty Lewis,' she said. 'As I came in.'

He made no comment. Still he didn't look up at her. She bit her lip angrily. 'Was it about Dassinget?'

'You learned about that from your bed of sickness?'

'I heard about it when I went out,' she said. 'Guy Keaping told me. I happened to meet him.'

'Harley Street appears to have a somewhat magnetic appeal to these — ah — friends of yours.'

'That was not the only thing he told me,' she said, and was furious with herself as she heard the pettily triumphant note ringing in her voice. She knew she sounded just like a schoolgirl who'd answered correctly a question asked by the teacher, after others in the class had fallen down on it.

He got up from his desk and came round towards her slowly. He took a cigarette from the skull and lit it with deliberation. She knew he was taking his time simply to tantalize her, then he looked at her for the first time since she had come into the study through a cloud of cigarette smoke.

'As you have surmised,' he said, 'with that remarkable prescience for which you are notable, her visit was in connection with Dassinget's tragic end. In part, at any rate.'

Betty Lewis had sat where Miss Frayle was now, she had nervously fiddled with her handbag while she began to tell Dr. Morelle the reason for her unexpected appearance at the house in Harley Street. 'It's Bill Scott,' she had told him, 'he tried to commit suicide to-night. I got to his room just in time. Another five minutes and he'd have had it.'

'How did he attempt this rash act?'

'Gas fire. Luckily he happened to leave the key in the door, on the outside. I got to work on him, opened the window, and the rest of it. Gave him artificial respiration. Stuff I'd learned at first-aid. He came round in three or four minutes.'

'You are to be commended,' he had said to her, as she took the cigarette he'd offered with trembling fingers.

'I asked him why he'd tried to do it. He said it was over the Collins girl. When she died he just went to pieces. He was sure Dassinget had killed her, incidentally.'

And now Miss Frayle, listening to him, uttered a gasping cry as he went on and related to her what Betty Lewis had proceeded to confide in him.

'It was pure speculation on his part?' Dr. Morelle had said to Betty Lewis, and she had nodded her head.

'I was the only one who knew it was true,' she had said simply. 'And I was in love with him, insanely in love with him.'

A long silence had hung on the air while Dr. Morelle had regarded the other enigmatically. Then he said to her: 'He told you this of his own accord?'

'He couldn't resist bragging to me,' and bitterness crept into her tone, 'trying to make me think he was a god. He said he tried to drop her, but she wouldn't give him up. And she'd found out that he was blackmailing Guy Keaping. She tried to put pressure on him, and she signed her own death warrant.'

She had gone on to tell him what she'd told Bill Scott, how Dassinget had said, he hadn't intended to kill Carla Collins, it had been an accident. She had ended up by saying to Dr. Morelle in a flat voice: 'You can say I was under his spell. Blackmailer, murderer, if you like, I loved him. I'd never have given him away.'

'What has happened to make you change your mind?' he had said, watching her from beneath those hooded eyelids.

She had shrugged her drooping shoulders miserably. 'It was something I just couldn't go on bearing by myself, I suppose. And now he's dead, there's no point.' She'd smiled at him wanly. 'They say confession's good for the soul.'

Listening to all this now, Miss Frayle recalled the scene between Carla Collins and Dassinget, her appeal to Guy Keaping at Blackwood's party, as if she shared some secret with the two men. Now she knew what the girl had meant. 'What a terrible thing about Bill Scott,' she said. 'Trying to kill himself like that.'

It was not a particularly scintillating observation for her to have made, she knew, after the revelations Dr. Morelle had passed on to her. But she was so anxious to tell him what she had learned, that it was the best she could do, before she plunged into her own story.

But Dr. Morelle contemplatively inhaled his Le Sphinx and as the smoke drifted upwards, he watched it, with sombre eyes.

'There are some,' he said, before she could open her mouth, 'who are totally inadequate to the demands life makes upon them. They muddle along from one failure to the next, always sinking deeper into a trough of misery and depression. They are the potential suicides of the world. For them, clear, decisive action is impossible. Involved in miserable relationships, they can see no way out. To cut the ties, strike out and make a new start, is impossible for them. Better the known unhappiness than the frightening unknown future. They always hope for some miracle to free them from their wretched bondage. Yet often all that is needed is one strong decision, not too difficult for one to make.'

Miss Frayle couldn't quite decide to whom he was referring. Was it Bill Scott? Or was he really thinking of Betty Lewis, or Dassinget? She gave up trying to puzzle it out and used his words to launch herself. 'You can say that again,' she said. 'I mean, take Guy Keaping, what a mess he's got himself into.'

Dr. Morelle raised an eyebrow. This was the individual in whom Miss Frayle had apparently held in certain regard not to say affection, even. He recalled the account she had given over the dicta-phone last night of the proceedings at the house in Little Venice, and the impression she had conveyed to him that this man was a complicated personality, something of a charmer into the bargain.

He noted the blush that had swept across Miss Frayle's face as she hurried over her words.

'He was being blackmailed all right,' she said. 'He'd killed one of Dassinget's girl-friends in a car accident in France, and hadn't stayed to face the music. How low can a man get?'

'But I'd rather imagined you liked him?'

The blush deepened. Miss Frayle pushed her horn-rims which had slipped half-way down her tip-tilted nose back into place.

'I did,' she said. 'I felt he was a bit mixed-up, but then aren't we all — ?'

'I'm not aware that I am in that unfortunate state, Miss Frayle.'

'Oh, no, not you,' she said hastily. 'But you know what I mean. Anyway, the point is that he's — well — he was the one with the squeaky shoes all the time. He hit me over the head at Grove Mansions, when I went to see Dassinget. And why?'

'I can hardly wait to know the answer, my dear Miss Frayle.'

'Because he was scared Dassinget would reveal to me the sort of man Guy Keaping really was.' It occurred to her even as she said it, that this wasn't entirely satisfying as a motive for the attack on her, but she went on. 'And anyone who'd do that, strike down a defenceless woman — '

She saw his expression harden and was sure she had said all that was necessary. She sat silent, she could not help feeling a little elated at the effect her words were having upon him, elation that was overshadowed by the stabbing pang as she thought of Guy Keaping.

She watched Dr. Morelle turn away and go back to the desk, the planes of his face hard and lined in the desklamp's glow. He sat down, stubbing out his cigarette, he flipped the papers on his desk and his eyes narrowed into long slits. Then he began to say something and she hung upon his words.

Perhaps he was going to compliment her for the way she'd handled the situation when she'd learned that Keaping was her assailant? She could not prevent the shy anticipating little smile that started at the corners of her mouth.

What he said was: 'Inspector Hood quite missed you while you were recovering from your headache. He felt sure your assistance would have proved invaluable to us.' He flicked one of the papers. 'I may have omitted to mention that he and I paid a not unprofitable visit to Somerset House before proceeding to Grove Mansions.'

She stared at him. He went on to inform her how he'd accompanied

Inspector Hood to Dassinget's flat, and the discovery there of the newspaper-references to the two-year-old car accident in which the Morse girl had died.

Miss Frayle frowned with exasperation. So he'd known all along about Guy Keaping being blackmailed by Dassinget, and why. And he'd let her burble on as if she was telling him something new, sensational. Chagrin filled her, she made an ineffectual attempt to query what he was saying.

'Somerset House?' she said. 'This evening? But it closes at half-past four.'

He glanced at her with a mixture of condescension and pity. 'Have you ever known me to be deterred by locked doors and red tape,' he said, 'when I demand admittance?'

Her mouth opened a little as he went on. 'Perhaps you would contrive to shake off the trance into which you appear to have succumbed,' he said.

She shook her head free of the mental picture it held of him and the burly Inspector Hood browsing through wills and details of births and deaths, marriages. What on earth could he have discovered there among the shelves, musty with the long years which could have had any bearing on what filled her mind?

He was saying, his tone sharp: 'Telephone Inspector Hood, I rather fancy the hour approaches for decisive action.'

23

The following morning lay damp and mild over Radio House, the streets were dull and autumnal. London's trees were beginning to stand skeletal against the sky. Inside Radio House, in the chief engineer's office, Dr. Morelle and Miss Frayle, together with Inspector Hood were listening to the chief engineer's soft Scottish accent as he said:

'It will follow the ordinary transmission at ten-thirty,' and he glanced at the inevitable clock high in the wall. 'Studio four you'll be. We'll tie you up to a recording channel.'

Inspector Hood gave him a nod. 'Much obliged to you,' he said. He, too, looked at the clock. 'We've got nearly ten minutes.'

Miss Frayle heard herself swallow, felt the palms of her hands moisten. This wasn't the first occasion when she had participated in this sort of strategem. Dr. Morelle possessed an enviable flair for staging an encounter with a suspect, one or more, which would result in shocked collapse, followed by a true confession from the appropriate party.

This time it would be different. This time she would be personally involved in the trapping of someone she knew closely.

'Ten-thirty the Crippen trailer goes out from studio four,' the chief engineer was saying. 'A five-minute spot, perfectly straightforward. An announcer, that's all. Plus there has to be the producer in charge. Guy Keaping.'

Miss Frayle listened, dumbly, her eyes held by Dr. Morelle's. The Scottish accent went on, itemising the procedure.

'End of the broadcast the announcer will leave the studio. But Guy Keaping,' and she heard herself swallow again, three pairs of eyes turned on her, 'will be held in conversation by you. Not in the control room, in the studio itself. The microphones will be up, unknown to him, and your conversation will be recorded in an adjacent recording room.'

How was she going through with it? she wondered miserably. How could she?

'The studio engineer in charge of the broadcast,' Dr. Morelle said to her, 'will be suitably instructed to see that the microphones are turned up full when you go through into the studio.' His eyes bored into hers mesmerically, the chief engineer gave a nod. 'Inspector Hood and I will be listening in the recording room.'

'I'm afraid I'm being a bit stupid,' she said bitterly. 'But I don't see the reason for all this, even now.'

Dr. Morelle merely smiled at her, frostily patronizing. Inspector Hood paced about the office. The chief engineer looked from one to the other questioningly. There seemed nothing more to be said. He eyed the clock. It said ten-twenty-five.

'Good luck,' the Scottish accent said, and the chief engineer went out of the office. After a few moments, the man from Scotland Yard followed him. When Inspector Hood had gone, Dr. Morelle looked at Miss Frayle.

'Trust me,' he said. 'All will work out for the best.'

She flashed him a grateful look. There

were moments, rare perhaps, when he revealed an unerring understanding of her emotions. 'It's like a nightmare,' she said.

'Some nightmares end in waking,' he said.

She went out of the office and made her way along to studio four. She looked out of a window as she passed. Down below buses, taxis, hurrying crowds. A newspaper-seller on the opposite corner. A bookstall with a man lazily thumbing through magazines. A girl walking along slowly, peeling the cellophane from a box of chocolates and starting to munch them.

Miss Frayle eyed the scene, abstract-edly, engulfed in her own private crisis. She looked up at the dull sky, then headed resolutely for studio four. As she went into the control room, Guy Keaping turned and looked at her, his face full of astonishment, and then he gave her that warm smile she knew so well.

'Pleasant surprise,' he said, 'and all that. But what's this in aid of?'

She had her answer prepared. 'I came

along with the boss,' she said frankly. 'He and Inspector Hood are nosing around. Thought I'd look in to see how you were managing without me.'

His expression clouded at once. A great surge of pity welled up within her. 'I didn't expect we'd seen the last of the bloodhounds,' he said. 'Anyway,' with an attempt at nonchalance, 'it's giving the newspapers something to write about. A murder a day and Radio House types at that. What could be juicier?'

It was Doug Blackwood who came in and began adjusting the microphone-level.

He appeared cool enough, anyway, Miss Frayle thought, as he said: 'Slumming, Miss Frayle?' So he was in charge, and she wondered how much Dr. Morelle or Inspector Hood had taken him into their confidence. Or if it had been decided to let him find out for himself as the trap snapped shut on the suspect? She smiled at him and included Guy Keaping when she said: 'May I stay while this goes out?'

The two of them grinned at her, a little

preoccupied, however. She knew that whatever either of them were thinking, for the moment the thoughts of each were concentrated on the job of getting the broadcast out. She experienced that feeling of excitement and tenseness, as she had known it before.

Keaping had turned to Blackwood. 'Put the talk-back key down will you? I want to talk to the announcer.'

The other held the key down. Keaping leaned forward and spoke to the announcer who had just come in to the studio on the other side of the glass window. 'Keep it going, will you?' The man nodded and gave a thumbs up. Guy Keaping sat back. 'I know this moron. He always loses pace after the first half-minute.'

'He's a bad reader,' Blackwood said. 'Drops his voice at the end of sentences, I know.'

One minute to go.

Miss Frayle, heart thumping, her mind a maelstrom, sat watching the second hand of the clock tick round. The red light began to flash intermittently. Doug

Blackwood pressed the buzzer to tell control room he was ready.

Steady red. Go ahead. Blackwood gave it the green light. It started.

Miss Frayle sat there, hearing nothing of what the announcer was saying. It was incredible, she thought. Here she was just about to help unmask a brutal murderer, who might have added her to his list, and the suspect's whole attention was given to seeing that a pretty little trailer for a programme about another murderer, Crippen, went out according to schedule.

She was the only one who might have any worry on her mind. She knew she looked tense and anxious. She couldn't help herself. She endeavoured her utmost to channel her thoughts to what was to happen in the the studio after the broadcast was over.

The door of the control room was opening, and Betty Lewis pushed her head round the door. 'Hello?' she said. 'Can I come in?'

Blackwood looked round, gave her an appraising grin. She saw Miss Frayle and stared at her in surprise. 'I thought you'd escaped from this loony bin,' she said, 'and gone back to your boss?'

'I have,' Miss Frayle said, 'he's here.'

'Oh,' the other said quietly. 'Yes, of course.' Guy Keaping looked curiously at the girl who said: 'Got a cigarette, anyone? That's what I'm here for.'

Guy Keaping, without taking his concentration off the man before the microphone found a packet of cigarettes. He handed them round to Betty Lewis, who took one, and Miss Frayle was praying that the woman would go. There had got to be no spanner in the works now.

But Betty Lewis stayed, chatting in an undertone to Blackwood. Miss Frayle's taut nerves were stretched to breaking point. Keaping muttered under his breath.

'Hell, he's running slow.' He made hurry-up signs to the man in the studio, who seemed to sense it and quickened his delivery. Keaping looked anxiously at the clock. It was going to be a race against time. No one spoke. The moments ticked by. For those on the programme it was just another one that could go wrong, that could over-run; for Miss Frayle it was an aeon to be lived through.

The announcer made it with ten seconds to spare. Blackwood gave a whistle of thankfulness, turned the microphone off, buzzed out. Guy Keaping leaned back in his chair, swearing. 'I'd like to flay him, one of these days,' he said bitterly. 'Does it every time.'

He got up and went through into the studio.

Betty Lewis said she'd better push off, but waited in the control room. Blackwood and Miss Frayle looked at each other. 'Good luck, Miss Frayle,' he said softly.

So he knew the part she was going to play, he'd been told that much. She stared at the stooped frame, while with a deft flick of a muscular wrist he turned up all the microphone knobs on his control-desk. At once Keaping's voice came through to them, his usually equable tones sharp with anger. He was telling off the announcer for the ragged job he'd just done. The other replied indifferently and they could hear his script rustle as he collected up the pages.

Miss Frayle's mouth was dry. She stood up, heard herself try to say something to Blackwood. Her voice was a rasp. 'Here I go,' she said, and went through into the studio.

Guy Keaping broke off, as she came in. He said abruptly to the other man: 'You'd better push off,' and the man walked out giving Miss Frayle a sickly grin. Keaping sighed and turned to her. 'I lost my temper, and it won't make a blind bit of difference.'

He moved about the studio, allowing his irritability to wear off, picking up the acoustic screens and arranging them differently.

She could hear her heart thumping, and she felt sick with mingled dread and remorse. She looked up at the wide window and saw Doug Blackwood staring down at her. She found a little courage in his expression, his strength seemed to reach her through the heavy plate glass. She glanced at the man beside her, her tongue moistening her dry mouth. 'Those shoes,' she heard herself say. 'Make a terrible squeak, don't they?'

He stopped dead, turned to her smiling, faintly surprised. 'Do they? I hadn't noticed.'

'It's a sound you'd never forget, once you've heard it.'

'So I'll have to have something done about it, won't I?'

'I think it's a bit too late,' she said. 'Now.'

His grin faded, he caught the tension in her voice. 'What's on your mind, kid?' he said lightly.

'I've remembered where I heard it the first time.'

'You're making it sound very mysterious.' He moved closer to her.

She knew she was trembling violently. She longed to turn on her heel and rush out. She could feel Blackwood's gaze on the nape of her neck, and she forced herself to speak. 'First time I heard it was yesterday, at Grove Mansions. When you followed me up the stairs.'

'Go on,' he was watching her, his

long chin thrust forward, his shoulders hunched.

'It was you. It was you who knocked me out. Wasn't it?'

He exploded in sudden anger. 'You seriously think I could do a thing like that? To you? You must be out of your mind.'

She saw with surprise that his hands were shaking. She started to raise her voice at him, but he cut her short.

'Since you know so much, and all of it wrong, you'd better have the truth,' he said. 'I did follow you up the stairs, because I wanted to stop you. I told you before you went in that he was dangerous. But he'd already seen you arrive. From his window. Seen you talking to me. He was waiting for you, by the emergency stairs. He called to you and you went to see who it was, he socked you, and if you ask me, serve you bloody well right, Miss Nosey Frayle.'

She clenched her fists with anger and mortification. She knew he was speaking the truth. She had been hideously wrong.

'I got up there a moment later,' he was

saying, 'just as he was hiding you in the cupboard. He told me to keep my mouth shut, or else. I was powerless.' His eyes turned away from her in his shame. 'He swore you'd only been knocked out, you'd be none the worse for it.'

'I'm glad you were happy about me,' she said.

He winced. 'I warned you,' he said. 'He knew you were mixed up with Dr. Morelle and the cops. He thought you were on to something. He had quite a bit to hide away one way and another.'

'So you cleared off and left me with him, I suppose?'

'Yes, I did,' he said miserably. 'It was a lousy thing to do. But I was sure you were okay really. It's the truth.' The words burst from him as if wrung out by torture. His face was twisted with self-hatred. 'You've got to believe me. If I tell you I made him pay for it later, will you believe me then?'

'What do you mean?' she said.

He drew a long shuddering breath. 'I went into his office and told him what I thought about him. The way he'd

311

attacked you. He came at me, and I bashed him one.'

'You killed him?' Miss Frayle said, and her voice was anguished. 'You did it, it was you all the time.'

24

Guy Keaping was staring at her. 'What do you mean?' He said it slowly, his face a few inches from hers, his eyes blazing.

Miss Frayle backed away from him. Blackwood's voice sounded in her ear: 'Need any help, Miss Frayle?'

She turned round with a gasp. Keaping was scowling darkly. 'What the hell do you want?' he said to Doug Blackwood.

'You sounded as if you weren't getting on too well together,' the other said with a lazy grin at the microphone.

'Keep out of this, blast you,' Keaping said. 'This has nothing to do with you.'

There were voices behind them. The studio door burst open and Dr. Morelle came in, followed by Inspector Hood. Next came the plain-clothes sergeant, and behind him the chief engineer. 'Quite a party,' Keaping said, sneering.

'Tell them the truth,' Miss Frayle said to him, 'You must tell them the truth.'

Perhaps she had been wrong about him knocking her unconscious. But that didn't matter. She could see in Inspector Hood's face what did matter. Dassinget's murderer. Dr. Morelle hadn't made any mistake, she could be sure of that. And it wasn't because she'd suffered a nasty headache that he was there with the detectives.

Guy Keaping looked from her to the others, his gaze hunted. He glanced at the microphone, before which he'd been standing with Miss Frayle. He knew that every word he'd said had been heard by the others. 'You think I killed Dassinget?' he said to Dr. Morelle. 'That's what you are here for really, you don't have to tell me.' He looked at Miss Frayle. 'But I didn't,' he said. 'I only knocked him out, I tell you. I only gave the blackmailing swine what he deserved.' He swung round upon Inspector Hood who had edged towards him. 'It's the truth,' he said, his voice was loud and harsh, 'just as I told her the truth about what happened at Grove Mansions.'

Inspector Hood regarded him gravely.

'I know what you told me, Mr. Keaping.'

'And it was all corroborated,' Keaping shouted at him in desperation. Miss Frayle's heart contracted with pity for him. 'Bill Scott, he saw me go in to see Dassinget. He saw me come out, before he went in himself — '

He broke off suddenly, the blood seemed to run out of his face, he took a step backwards. 'That bit isn't true, I admit it,' he said in a hollow mutter. 'I didn't see him actually go in, but I was sure he was going in to see Dassinget. He said so himself. I thought he'd found him as I'd left him, and that he'd denied it because he'd chucked him out of the window.'

'He denies that he even saw him,' Inspector Hood said gruffly. 'He can't be shaken on that.'

'Whether you assumed that he did,' Dr. Morelle said quietly, 'or lied in the hope of implicating him, is a matter for your conscience. You say Dassinget was alive when you left him? That you'd merely knocked him unconscious?'

Guy Keaping shot a look at him. A

little colour began to steal back into his face. 'I swear it,' he said. 'I killed someone once, by accident, you know all about that. I couldn't murder anyone, even Dassinget.'

There was such contrition in his voice that Miss Frayle felt reassured once more, and looking at Inspector Hood, was he regarding Guy Keaping as if he intended to slip handcuffs on him? As for Dr. Morelle, he appeared as saturninely urbane as ever. Yet, while she observed that the tension in his attitude had begun to relax, she sensed an increased tautness in the studio.

'The young woman, Betty Lewis,' Dr. Morelle said, 'expressed the view to me that confession is good for the soul. She was not far wrong; and I might add that it is also contagious. Given an appropriate setting and sufficient inducement.' He glanced round him. 'And what could be more suitable than this? This quiet, almost clinical atmosphere is as suitable almost as my own study. And with you, Miss Frayle, to lure the suspect on.'

Miss Frayle shifted uneasily from one

foot to another and looked shamefacedly at Guy Keaping. Dr. Morelle had made a fool out of her again, and with deliberate intention. Malice aforethought, she might say.

The cool incisive voice continued.

'So far, we have managed fairly satisfactorily,' Dr. Morell said. 'You,' with a probing look at Guy Keaping, 'have filled in part of the jigsaw. It remains for the final pieces to be fitted into place. Of course, there remains the other suspects. You were an obvious one.'

Keaping made a restless movement. 'Bill Scott was another,' Dr. Morelle said, 'for equally obvious reasons. There was the young woman I have just mentioned, Betty Lewis. Her motive was not so obvious, but paradoxically it could be none the less powerful. Her motive for wanting Dassinget dead might have been a secret one which none could have suspected.'

'Only thing,' Inspector Hood said, in a quiet mutter, 'is that she'd have to lift him up and shove him through the window. While he was unconscious, a dead weight.

She doesn't look the sort of girl you'd expect to have the strength.'

Dr. Morelle nodded as if in agreement. Then he said: 'But anger and hatred, passion or fear can provide even a relatively weak young woman with momentarily fearsome power.'

The atmosphere of the studio, brightly lit and metallic, became even tenser. Miss Frayle glanced at the window, but couldn't see Betty Lewis.

'But might we not consider someone else?' Dr. Morelle said, and Miss Frayle exhaled a low hiss. Inspector Hood had clamped his cold pipe between his teeth. 'Someone whose motive was quite different from these three, whose devotion to Carla Collins went deeper even than the man, Scott's.'

Miss Frayle gave a sudden gasp of astonishment, she caught a movement out of the corner of her eye. It was someone beside her. 'Who was bound to her,' Dr. Morelle's voice was inexorable, 'not by the bonds of love, perhaps, but remorse, and who sought to expiate his own sins by revenging her death. Who had, in fact, married her.'

'Who?' Guy Keaping said, his voice rasping.

Again that movement beside her and Miss Frayle jerked her head round as Doug Blackwood stepped forward.

'You're right, Dr. Morelle,' he said. 'This is as good a time and place for me to throw my confession into the hat.'

He kept his tone light, he might have been good-humouredly discussing some technical matter connected with a broadcast programme. But Miss Frayle saw that his face was granite hard, the neck set upon the wide, muscular shoulders was thrust forward, so that a vein stood out. Betty Lewis must have gone, she decided idly.

'I went into Dassinget's office,' he said. 'It must have been just after you'd gone,' he looked at Keaping. 'I saw Bill Scott disappearing round the corner, I thought he'd just come out. He didn't see me. There was Dassinget on the floor, out cold. The office was in a shambles. I thought Bill Scott must have had more guts than I'd given him credit for. He'd followed through with his threat to beat up the swine, that was what I thought, and I was grateful to him.' He gave Dr. Morelle a glance. 'I talked too much yesterday evening,' he said. 'I didn't realize I had.'

Dr. Morelle spread out his hands. 'You didn't realize to whom you were talking,' he said softly.

The heavy shoulders gave a shrug. 'It's a weight off my mind,' Doug Blackwood said. 'One of the many I've carried too long. I married Carla out of gratitude for what her mother had done for me, after her mother died. It didn't work out. How could it? We separated, but I still felt I owed her much more than I could ever repay.' He grinned at Dr. Morelle. 'Bound to her as you put it, not by any bond of love, but by remorse for the mess I've made of my life.'

Miss Frayle recalled Dr. Morelle's words to her last night. About those who muddle into one failure after another. The potential suicides; and potential murderers, too, she realized. She knew Dr. Morelle's view that suicide and murderer were not so different, they all sought their self-destruction in the long run. She sighed, as Doug Blackwood went on:

'But, of course, Dr. Morelle, you know all about that. You only had to peep into your crystal to see what I'd left out last night, so you could make two and two add up to four.'

'It was Somerset House,' Inspector Hood said shortly. 'It told us all we needed to know.'

'As simple as that?' Blackwood's frame seemed to sag. He passed a hand wearily over his face. 'I don't know if I meant to kill Dassinget when I went to his office. Then when I saw him like that, it seemed too good to be true. I got him up by the arms, lifted him, he was starting to come round, and I pushed him out. I left the office fast and went back to the studio. It had all happened so quickly.' He gave a dry, crackling laugh. 'It worked out for me. I'd have got away with it, if it hadn't been for you, Dr. Morelle. It'll teach me never to let a psychiatrist buy me a drink.'

Dr. Morelle watched him sombrely as

Doug Blackwood moved towards Inspector Hood. The plain-clothes man was on the other side of him and they moved out of the studio together.

At the door Blackwood turned to Guy Keaping. 'I hope they got that on tape as well as your stuff with Miss Frayle,' he said. 'Even though I shan't hear it played back.'

He went out between the others.

The chief engineer followed them. With a choking sensation and her horn-rims misted, Miss Frayle moved towards Guy Keaping. Dr. Morelle went slowly to the door, speaking to her over his shoulder. 'There is nothing else for us to do here,' he said.

She hesitated, then gave the figure beside her a quick glance. He was smiling at her with the same warm smile she remembered so well.

'I'm afraid there is, Dr. Morelle,' she said firmly. 'The least I can do is to buy Mr. Keaping a cup of coffee.'

Dr. Morelle turned very slowly and eyed her, his expression may have held surprise or exasperation, or both. Miss

Frayle didn't really care as she slipped her hand into Guy Keaping's.

Dr. Morelle hesitated a moment, then swung round and went out of the studio.

THE END

We do hope that you have enjoyed reading this large print book.

Did you know that all of our titles are available for purchase?

We publish a wide range of high quality large print books including:
Romances, Mysteries, Classics
General Fiction
Non Fiction and Westerns

Special interest titles available in large print are:
The Little Oxford Dictionary
Music Book, Song Book
Hymn Book, Service Book

Also available from us courtesy of Oxford University Press:
Young Readers' Dictionary
(large print edition)
Young Readers' Thesaurus
(large print edition)

For further information or a free brochure, please contact us at:
Ulverscroft Large Print Books Ltd.,
The Green, Bradgate Road, Anstey,
Leicester, LE7 7FU, England.
Tel: (00 44) **0116 236 4325**
Fax: (00 44) **0116 234 0205**

*Other titles in the
Linford Mystery Library:*

THE HARASSED HERO

Ernest Dudley

Murray Selwyn, six-foot-two and athletic, was so convinced he had not long to live that when he came across a hold-up, a murder and masses of forged fivers, he was too worried about catching a chill to give them much attention. But when he met his pretty nurse, Murray began to forget his ailments, and by the end of a breath-taking chase after some very plausible crooks, the hypochondriac had become a hero.

HELL HATH NO FURY

Rex Marlowe

Private investigator Sam Spain receives a visit from a little old lady, who wants him to find her twenty-two-year-old daughter, Irene, who has been missing for a month. Sam learns that Hugo Dare, a racketeer-turned-politician, has supplied Irene with a bungalow on Eucalyptus Drive. From the moment Sam discovers a corpse in Irene's room, he runs into nothing but grief. Irene is in a jam, framed for murder. Sam hides the girl and goes on with his investigation. Then he finds himself in the same jam as Irene — framed for a murder he hasn't committed!

A LONELY PLACE TO DIE

Colin Robertson

'The old lady — with a bustle.' These words, uttered by Vincent Stroud before he was murdered, set Peter Gayleigh once again on the adventure trail. He becomes interested in a remote castle in Scotland where something very odd appears to be going on. His determination to solve this mystery brings him into contact with Shirley Quentin whose father, the owner of the castle, has disappeared. Finally, on a Scottish moor, Gayleigh meets the Herr Doktor Ulrich von Shroeder, a biochemist and master spy.

THE POSSESSED

E. C. Tubb

In the remote Scottish Highlands there lurks a truly terrifying menace. It seems to be centred at a Government Research Establishment, but without definite proof of the exact nature of the menace, the authorities cannot act decisively. It was up to the ace detective, Martin Slade, to investigate and find that proof — even at the cost of his own life!

THE SISKIYOU TWO-STEP

Richard Hoyt

John Denson, a private investigator, goes to Oregon's North Umpqua River to fish trout but, instead, he finds himself caught up in a net of international intelligence agents and academics. It all starts when the naked body of a girl with a bullet hole between her eyes goes rushing past Denson in the rapids. He embarks on a bizarre search to find the girl's identity and to bring her killer to justice. Strange clues lead to three more corpses, and only the Siskiyou Two-Step saves Denson from being the fourth . . .

THREE MAY KEEP A SECRET

Stella Phillips

The proudest citizens of Dolph Hill would not deny that it was a backwater where nothing ever happened — until, that is, the arrival of handsome, secretive Peter Markland disturbs the surface. After his shocking and violent death, old secrets begin to emerge. Detectives Matthew Furnival and Reg King are put on the case. As they delve through the conflicting mysteries, how will they arrive at the one relevant truth?